He pulled her  away from the into the field collapsed, arm around each other.

His eyes met hers. "I thought I'd lost you," he whispered.

She took his face in both hands and pressed her lips to his, the kiss desperate in its intensity. Everything receded, burned away by passion.

He was the first to pull away, breaking the kiss. "You're the most amazing woman," he said.

"You're making a habit of saving my life," she said.

His expression hardened and he dropped his hand. "You don't owe me anything."

"This isn't about debts and payments," she said.

"Then what is it about?"

"It's about you making me feel more alive than I have in years. It's about...I don't know." She looked away. She had almost said *love*, but that was absurd.

"Maybe it doesn't matter why right now," he said. He pulled her close again.

SAVED BY THE SHERIFF

—

CINDI MYERS

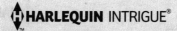

HARLEQUIN INTRIGUE®

For Lucy

Recycling programs
for this product may
not exist in your area.

ISBN-13: 978-1-335-63926-4

Saved by the Sheriff

Copyright © 2018 by Cynthia Myers

Printed in U.S.A.

Cindi Myers is the author of more than fifty novels. When she's not crafting new romance plots, she enjoys skiing, gardening, cooking, crafting and daydreaming. A lover of small-town life, she lives with her husband and two spoiled dogs in the Colorado mountains.

Visit the Author Profile page at Harlequin.com.

CAST OF CHARACTERS

Lacy Milligan—Wrongfully convicted of murdering her boss, Lacy has spent the last three years in prison. Free at last, she'd like to find the real murderer in order to completely clear her name, but tracking him down puts her in danger—and means relying on the one man she has sworn to hate.

Sheriff Travis Walker—Putting away a murderer helped win the handsome young deputy the election for sheriff. He carries the guilt of having helped convict the wrong person and now feels obligated to protect Lacy to try to make up for his mistake. But his feelings toward her are more than merely protective.

Andy Stenson—The young lawyer's murder shocked the small town of Eagle Mountain. No one will truly rest easy until his murderer is found.

Brenda Stenson—Andy's widow still grieves her husband, but the investigation is revealing a side of him that shocks her, and could put her in danger.

Henry Hake—The real estate developer hired Andy Stenson to help him put through a luxury resort development that wasn't welcomed by locals. Was Andy murdered because he helped Hake—or because he knew too much about Hake's business dealings?

Jan Selkirk—The former Eagle Mountain mayor knows more about the case than she's willing to admit.

Ian Barnes—The climbing guide and newcomer to town is attracting a lot of attention from local women, but he's more interested in Lacy than she would like.

Alvin Exeter—The writer is supposedly working on a book about Lacy, and Andy Stenson's murder, with or without her cooperation.

Chapter One

Lacy Milligan flinched as the heavy steel door clanged shut behind her. After almost three years, that sound still sent a chill through her. She reminded herself she wouldn't ever have to hear that sound again after today. Today she was a free woman.

She followed the guard down the gleaming tiled hallway, the smell of disinfectant stinging her nose. At the door to a reception room at the front of the building she stopped and waited while a second guard unlocked and opened the door. Her lawyer, Anisha Cook, stood on the other side, beaming. She pulled Lacy to her in a hug and Lacy stiffened. That was something else she would have to get used to—being touched. Touching wasn't allowed in prison—even something as simple as a hug could lead to extra searches, even punishment. But those rules didn't apply to her anymore, she reminded herself, and awkwardly returned the other woman's embrace. Anisha, still smiling, released her, and Lacy noticed there were other people in the room—the warden, reporters, her parents.

"Lacy, what are your feelings, now that your conviction has been overturned?" A sandy-haired man shoved a microphone at her.

"I'm happy, of course," she said. "Ready to go home."

"Do you have anything to say to Rayford County Sheriff Travis Walker?" another reporter asked.

So Travis was the sheriff now. Putting a murderer behind bars had probably earned him points with the right people in town. Except he had arrested the wrong person. "I don't have anything to say to him," she said.

"Even though he's the one who came forward with the evidence that cleared your name?" the reporter asked.

Travis had done that? She shot a look at Anisha, who nodded. Lacy would have to get the whole story from her later. "That doesn't make up for the three years I spent behind bars for a crime I didn't commit," Lacy said. Three years of her life she would never get back.

"What are your plans now that you're free?" the sandy-haired reporter asked.

Plans? Plans were something a person with a

future made—something Lacy hadn't had until yesterday, when word came down that she was to be released. She had been afraid to believe it was really going to happen until now. "I'm going to go home with my parents and consider my options," she said.

She caught her mother's eye across the room. Jeanette Milligan was openly weeping, tears running down her cheeks, while Lacy's dad held her tightly.

"We need to be going now," Anisha said. "We ask that you respect Lacy's privacy as she settles in." She put her arm around Lacy's shoulders and guided her toward the door.

Outside, her mother's green Subaru Outback waited—the same car she had had when Lacy had entered the Denver Women's Correctional Facility three years before. Lacy's dad embraced her and kissed her cheek, then it was her mother's turn. "I have your old room all ready for you," her mom said. "And we're having steak for dinner, and chocolate cake."

"Great, Mom." Lacy forced a smile. Moving back home had seemed the best choice right now, since she had almost no money and no job. It would only be temporary, until she figured out what she was going to do with the rest of her life and got back on her feet. But it still felt like going back in time while the rest of the world moved forward.

"We'll get together next week for coffee or something," Anisha said. "If you need anything before then, just call." She waved and headed for her own car, then Lacy slid into the back seat of her parents' car and they were off.

They tried to make small talk for a while, but soon fell silent. Lacy rested her head against the window and stared out at the summer-browned city landscape, which quickly gave way to the green foothills, and then the Rocky Mountains. Only five more hours until she was home in Eagle Mountain, the little resort town where her family had settled when Lacy was fourteen. Once upon a time, she had thought she would stay in Eagle Mountain forever, but now she wasn't so sure. Maybe there were too many bad memories there for her to ever be comfortable again.

Lacy slept, and woke only when her dad pulled the car into the driveway of the Victorian cottage just off Eagle Mountain's main street that had been their home for the past ten years. A lump rose in Lacy's throat as she studied the stone walkway that led up to the front porch that spanned the width of the house, with its white-painted posts and railings and lacelike gingerbread trim. The peonies under the railings were in full bloom, like big pink pom-poms filling the flower beds. A banner over the front steps declared Welcome Home Lacy!

She took her time getting out of the car, fighting the instinct to run up the steps and straight into her room. She was going to have to get used to facing people again, to dealing with their questions about what she had been through and what she planned to do next. She had never been good at that kind of thing, but she was going to have to find a way to cope.

She started up the walkway, but at the top of the steps, she noticed the uniformed man seated in the porch swing and froze. Travis Walker, all six feet of him, made even taller by the cowboy boots and Stetson he wore, stood and moved toward her. "What are you doing here?" Lacy asked, heart pounding madly. Had there been some mistake? Had he come to arrest her again?

Travis removed his hat, revealing thick brown hair that fell boyishly over his forehead. When Lacy had first met him in high school, she had thought he was the handsomest boy she had ever seen. Too much had passed between them for her to think that now. "I came to apologize," he said. "I know it doesn't make up for all I put you through, but I wanted to say I'm truly sorry. I've done what I can to make up for my mistakes."

"Your mistakes cost me three years of my life!" Lacy hated the way her voice broke on the words. "You humiliated me in front of everyone I knew. In front of people I've never even met. You accused me of the most horrible crime anyone could commit."

His face showed the strain he was feeling, his brown eyes pained. "I would give anything to take all of it back," he said. "But I can't. All I can do is say again that I'm sorry, and I hope you'll find it in your heart one day to forgive me."

"You don't deserve my forgiveness," she said, and rushed past him, tears stinging her eyes. She refused to break down in front of him.

She paused in the darkened living room, fighting for composure. Her father's quiet voice drifted to her through the opened screen door. "Give it a few days. This is hard for her—for all of us."

"I didn't mean to intrude on your first day back together," Travis said. "I just wanted her to know how I felt. It didn't seem right to wait any longer to apologize. It doesn't make up for anything, but it had to be said."

"And we appreciate it," her dad said. "We

appreciate all you've done for her. It says a lot about a man when he's willing to admit he was wrong."

"I'll leave you alone now," Travis said. "You deserve your privacy and I have a lot of work to do."

"Thank goodness there's not a lot of crime in Rayford County, but I imagine the job has its challenges," her dad said.

"It does," Travis said. "But right now my priority is finding out who really killed Andy Stenson. I know now that Lacy didn't kill him, but I have to bring to justice the person who did."

TRAVIS WALKED AWAY from the Milligan home, down the street shaded by tall evergreens and cottonwoods, up a block to Main. He liked that the town of Eagle Mountain—the only incorporated town in Rayford County—was small enough, and the sheriff's department centrally located enough, that he could walk almost anywhere. A big part of policing in a rural area like this was simply being a presence. Seeing uniforms on the street made people feel safer, and it made troublemakers think twice about acting up.

He passed under the large banner advertising Eagle Mountain Pioneer Days Festival, the biggest tourist attraction of the summer for the little town, with a parade and fireworks, outdoor concerts, crafts booths and anything else the town council could think of that would entertain people and induce them to stay a few days and spend money.

"Sheriff!"

He turned to see Mayor Larry Rowe striding toward him. Solidly built and energetic, Rowe was a relative newcomer to town who, after a year on the county planning committee, had spent a significant amount of money on his campaign for mayor two years ago—unusual in a town where most public officials ran unopposed. "Mayor." Travis stopped and waited for the older man to catch up.

"Sheriff, I wanted to talk to you about security for the festival," Rowe said.

"We'll have plenty of officers patrolling," Travis said. "I'm putting all of the reserves on duty, and as many of the full-time staff as possible."

Rowe nodded. "We don't want any trouble to detract from the festivities." He stared down the street, in the direction Travis had come. "I understand Lacy Milligan is back in town."

"Yes, I stopped by to see her."

"Oh?" The lines on either side of Rowe's mouth deepened. "How is she?"

"She's still processing everything that's happened, I think."

"I hope she doesn't have any plans to sue the city," Rowe said. "I'll have to consult our attorney, prepare for that possibility."

"I don't think she has any plans to sue," Travis said.

"Do whatever you can to see that she doesn't. I have to go now. You'll keep me posted if any problems arise with the Milligans."

"Yes, sir."

The mayor moved on, and Travis resumed the walk to his office. Though he didn't consider Rowe a friend, he appreciated that the mayor rarely involved himself in the operation of the sheriff's department. Travis was free to do his job as he saw fit.

A ten-minute stroll took Travis back to the office. His office manager, sixty-eight-year-old Adelaide Kinkaid, who refused to even consider retiring—and was sharper than most thirty-year-olds—looked up from her computer screen. "How did it go?" she asked.

"About like I expected." Travis hung his Stetson on the rack by the door. "She told me I'd ruined her life and tried not to let me see she was crying." He shrugged. "In her place, I'd probably feel the same way. I guess I'm lucky she didn't punch me."

"You're already beating yourself up enough," Adelaide said.

"Why are you beating yourself up?" Deputy Gage Walker, Travis's younger brother, emerged from his office. Taller than Travis by two inches and lighter than him by twenty pounds, Gage looked like the basketball forward he had been in high school, lean and quick.

"I went over to see Lacy Milligan," Travis said.

Gage's face sobered. "Ouch! That took guts."

"It was the least she deserved. Not that she thinks so."

"You did what you could," Gage said. "Now the ball is in her court."

"Not exactly."

"What do you mean?" Gage asked.

"I mean, I still have to find Andy Stenson's killer. And doing that will be easier with her help."

"Wait a minute—you proved she was innocent—but you think she knows something?" Gage asked.

"She can at least walk me through Andy's records, tell me about his clients. She was his only employee. She may have encountered his murderer, without knowing it."

"What about Andy's widow?" Adelaide asked.

"Brenda knows nothing about the business," Travis said. "She's told me everything she knows, but it's not enough. I need Lacy to help me."

"And I need a million dollars," Gage said. "But I'm not going to get it."

Travis moved into his office and dropped into his chair behind his desk, staring at the stack of papers in his inbox, thinking about Lacy. She was the first murderer he had ever arrested—the only one, actually. He was a deputy with only a few years on the force at the time, and murder was a rare crime in Rayford County. Sheriff's department calls ran more toward theft, vandalism, domestic violence and what he thought of as tourist calls—lost hikers, lost wallets, lost dogs and people who had locked themselves out of their cars.

The murder of young attorney Andy Stenson had been a shock to everyone, but the chief suspect had been pretty clear. Lacy Milligan's prints had been found on the murder weapon, she had been overheard arguing with Andy that afternoon and someone had seen a woman who matched Lacy's description—from her build to her dark hair—outside the office shortly before the time of Andy's death.

Travis hadn't wanted to believe Lacy was a killer. She had always been the pretty, quiet girl in high school. After she had graduated high school and had gone to work for Andy, Travis had occasionally seen her downtown and they would say hello. He had even thought about asking her out, but had never gotten around to it.

But then Andy had died and the only evidence Travis could find pointed to Lacy. She hadn't been able to produce anyone who could confirm her alibi—that she had been almost two hours away at her cousin's basketball game. The cousin hadn't seen her there, and no one else could remember her being there. And then the prosecutor had discovered funds missing from the law firm's account, and a deposit in almost the same amount in Lacy's account.

The jury had deliberated only a few hours before handing down a conviction. Travis had felt sick as he watched the bailiff lead Lacy from court, but he had been convinced he had done his job. He had found a murderer.

And then, only two months ago, he had been whiling away the time online and had come across a video someone had posted of a college basketball game—a game in which a promising young player—now a major NBA star—had made a series of free throws that hinted at his future greatness. Watching the video, Travis had recognized a familiar face on the sidelines.

Lacy Milligan—a smiling, carefree Lacy—had stared out at him from the screen. A time stamp on the video corroborated her story of being at her cousin's game. Further research backed this up. Here was her alibi. When Andy Stenson was stabbed in the heart, Lacy Milligan was two hours away.

From there, the rest of the evidence began to fall apart. Travis hired a former detective to review the case and the detective—who had retired to Eagle Mountain after a storied career with the Los Angeles Police Department—determined that what had looked like missing funds was merely a bookkeeping error, and the deposit in Lacy's account was, as she had said, the proceeds from the sale of some jewelry she had inherited.

Travis had felt sick over the error. He hadn't been able to eat or sleep as he worked feverishly to see that the decision in the case was vacated. He also did what he could to publicize his efforts to clear the name of the woman he had wronged. He wanted everyone to know that Lacy was innocent.

Now she was home. He didn't blame her for hating him, though it hurt to see the scorn in her eyes. All he knew to do now was to work even harder to find the real killer.

The phone rang and he heard Adelaide answer. A moment later, his extension buzzed. "Sheriff, it's for you," Adelaide said. "It's George Milligan."

Lacy's dad. Travis snatched up the receiver. "Mr. Milligan, how can I help you?"

"I think you need to come over here, Sheriff." George Milligan's voice held the strain of someone who had taken almost more than he could bear. "We've had a, well, I'm not sure how to describe it. An incident."

Travis sat up straighter, his stomach knotting. "What's happened? Is someone hurt? Is Lacy hurt?"

"Someone threw a rock through our front window." George's voice broke. "It had a...a note tied to it. Just one word on the note—*murderer.*"

"I'll be right over," Travis said. Hadn't these people suffered enough? Hadn't they all suffered enough?

Chapter Two

Lacy stared at the grapefruit-sized chunk of red granite that sat in the middle of the library table beneath the front window of her family home, shards of glass like fractured ice scattered about it. Strands of thin wire held the note in place, a single word scrawled crookedly in red marker, like an accusation made in blood.

Murderer! She had worn the label for three years, but she would never get used to it. Seeing it here, in the place she had thought of as a refuge, when she had believed her ordeal over, hurt more than she had imagined. Worse, the word hurt her parents, who had put their own lives on hold, and even mortgaged their home, to save her.

A black-and-white SUV pulled into the driveway and Lacy watched out the window as Travis Walker slid out of the vehicle and strode up the walkway to the door. Everything about him radiated competence and authority, from his muscular frame filling out the crisp lines of his brown sheriff's uniform to the determined expression on his handsome face. When he said something was right, it must be right. So when he had said she had murdered Andy Stenson, everyone had believed him. Men like Travis didn't make mistakes.

Except he had.

The doorbell rang and her father opened it and ushered Travis inside. Lacy steeled herself to face him. Travis hadn't thrown the rock through her parents' window, but as far as she was concerned, he was to blame.

"Hello, Lacy." Ever the gentleman, Travis touched the brim of his hat and nodded to her.

She nodded and took a step back, away from the rock—and away from him. He walked over and looked down at the projectile, his gaze taking in the broken window, the shattered glass and the note. He leaned closer to study the note. "Has anything like this happened before?" he asked.

It took her a moment to realize he had addressed the question to her. She shrugged. "Not really. There were a few letters to the editor in the paper during my trial, and a few times when I would walk into a place and everyone would stop talking and stare at me."

"But no direct threats or name calling?" he asked.

She shook her head. "No."

"I can't understand why anyone would do this now." Her father joined them. Her mother was upstairs, lying down with a headache. "Lacy has been cleared. Everyone knows that."

"Maybe not everyone." Travis straightened. "I'll get an evidence kit from my car. Maybe we'll get some fingerprints off the note."

Lacy doubted whoever threw that rock would be stupid enough to leave fingerprints, but she didn't bother arguing. Travis went outside and stopped on the sidewalk to survey the flower bed. Maybe he was looking for footprints? Or maybe he liked flowers.

He returned a few moments later, wearing latex gloves and carrying a cardboard box. He lifted the rock and settled it in the box. "In order to hurl the rock through the window like this, whoever threw it would have to be close—either standing on the porch or in the flower beds," he said, as he taped up the box and labeled it. "I didn't see any footprints in the flower beds, or disturbed plants, so I'm guessing porch. Did you see or hear anyone?"

"We were all in the back of the house, preparing dinner in the kitchen," her father said.

"I'll talk to the neighbors, see if any of them

saw anything," Travis said. "After the window shattered, did you hear anything—anyone running away, or a car driving away?"

"No," her father said.

Both men looked at Lacy. "No," she said. "I didn't hear anything."

"Who would do something like this?" her father asked. His face sagged with weariness, and he looked years older. Guilt made a knot in Lacy's stomach. Even though she hadn't thrown the rock, she was the target. She had brought this intrusion into her parents' peaceful life. Maybe moving back home had been a bad idea.

"I don't know," Travis said. "There are mean people in the world. Obviously, someone doesn't believe Lacy is innocent."

"The paper has run articles," her father said. "It's been on all the television stations—I don't know what else we can do."

"You can help me find the real murderer."

He was addressing Lacy, not her dad, his gaze pinning her. She remembered him looking at her that way the day he arrested her, the intensity of his stare making it clear she wasn't going to get away with not answering his questions.

"Why should I help you?" she asked.

"You worked closely with Andy," he said. "You knew his clients. You can walk me through his records. I'm convinced he knew his murderer."

"What if you try to pin this on the wrong person again?"

He didn't even flinch. "I won't make that mistake again."

"Honey, I think maybe Travis is right," her father said. "You probably know more about Andy's job than anyone."

"What about Brenda?" Lacy asked. "She was his wife. He would have told her if someone was threatening him before he told me."

"He never said anything like that to her," Travis said. "And she doesn't know anything about his law practice."

"I'm pretty sure all the files from the business are still in storage," she said. "You don't need my help going through them."

"I do if I'm going to figure out what any of it means. You can help me avoid wasting time on irrelevant files and focus on anything that might be important."

His intense gaze pinned her, making her feel trapped. She wanted to say no, to avoid having anything to do with him. But what if he was right and he needed her help to solve the case? What if, by doing nothing, she was letting the real killer get away with murder? "All right," she said. "I'll help you."

"Thank you. I'll call you tomorrow or the next day and set up a time to get together." He picked up the box with the rock, touched the brim of his hat again and left.

Lacy sank into a nearby arm chair. This wasn't how she had envisioned her homecoming. She had hoped to be able to put the past behind her once and for all. Now she was volunteering to dive right back into it.

TRAVIS CRUISED EAGLE MOUNTAIN'S main street, surveying the groups of tourists waiting for tables at Kate's Kitchen or Moe's Pub, the men filling the park benches outside the row of boutiques, chatting while they waited for their wives. He waved to Paige Riddell as he passed her bed-and-breakfast, drove past the library and post office, then turned past the Episcopal Church, the fire station and the elementary school before he turned toward his office. The rock someone had hurled through Lacy's front window sat in the box on the passenger seat, a very ordinary chunk of iron-ore-infused granite that could have come from almost any roadside or backyard in the area.

Who would hurl such a weapon—and its hateful message—through the window of a woman who had already endured too much because of mistakes made by Travis and others?

Eagle Mountain wasn't a perfect place, but it wasn't known for violent dissension. Disagreements tended to play themselves out in the form of letters to the editor of the local paper or the occasional shouting match after a few too many beers at one of the local taverns.

When Travis had arrested Lacy for the murder of Andy Stenson, he had received more than one angry phone call, and a few people had refused to speak to him ever since. When he had issued a public statement declaring Lacy's innocence, most people had responded positively, if not jubilantly, to the news. He couldn't recall hearing even a whisper from anyone that a single person believed Lacy was still a murderer.

On impulse, he drove past the police station and two blocks north, to the former Eagle Mountain Hospital, now home to the county Historical Society and Museum. As he had hoped, Brenda Stenson was just locking up for the day when Travis parked and climbed out of his SUV. "Hello, Travis," she said as she tucked the key into her purse. A slender blonde with delicate features and a smattering of freckles across her upturned nose, Brenda seemed to be regaining some of the vivacity that had all but vanished when her husband of only three years had been murdered. "What's up?"

"Lacy came home today," he said. "I was just over at her folks' place."

"How is she? I saw her mom yesterday and told her to tell Lacy I would stop by tomorrow—I thought maybe the family would like a little time alone before the crowds of well-wishers descend."

"So you don't have any problem with her being out?" Travis asked, watching her carefully.

She pushed a fall of long blond hair out of her eyes. "Lacy didn't kill Andy," she said. "I should have spoken on her behalf at the trial, but I was so torn up about Andy—it was all I could do to get out of bed in the morning. Later on..." She shrugged. "I didn't know what to think. I'm glad she's out."

"Except that now we don't know who is responsible for Andy's death," Travis said.

"No, we don't. It makes it hard to move on, but sometimes these things never get solved, do they? I hate to think that, but I'm trying to be realistic."

"I want to find the real murderer," Travis said. "I feel like I owe it to you and Andy—and to Lacy."

"You didn't try and convict her all by yourself," Brenda said. "And you fought harder than anyone to free her once you figured out the truth."

"But I started the ball rolling," he said. "And this isn't really going to be over for any of us until we find out what really happened that day."

She sighed. "So what's the next move?"

"I know we've been over this before, but humor me. Do you know of anyone who was angry or upset with Andy—about anything? An angry husband whose wife Andy represented in a divorce? A drunk driving case he lost?"

"Andy hadn't been practicing law long enough to make enemies," Brenda said. "And Eagle Mountain is a small town—I know pretty much everyone who was ever a client of his. None of them seem like a murderer to me."

"I think the odds that the killer was a random stranger are pretty low," Travis said. "So one of those nice local people is likely the murderer."

Brenda rubbed her hands up and down her arms, as if trying to warm herself. "It makes me sick to think about it," she said.

"If I can convince Lacy to help me, would you mind if we go through Andy's case files?" Travis asked. "I figure she would have known his clients almost as well as he did."

"Of course I don't mind. Everything is in

storage. I haven't had the heart to go through anything myself."

"I don't know if it will help, but it seems like a good place to start," he said.

"Stop by whenever you're ready and I'll give you the key to my storage unit," she said.

They said good-night and Travis returned to his SUV. He had just started the vehicle when his cell phone buzzed. "Hello?"

"Sheriff, Wade Tomlinson called to report a shoplifter at their store," Adelaide said. "He said he saw you drive past a few minutes ago and wondered if you could swing by."

"Tell him I'll be there in a couple of minutes." Travis ended the call and turned the SUV back toward Main, where Wade Tomlinson and Brock Ryan operated Eagle Mountain Outfitters, a hunting, fishing and climbing store that catered to locals and tourists alike. Technically, a call like this should have been routed through the countywide dispatch center. The dispatcher would then contact the appropriate department and the officer who was closest to the scene would respond. But locals were just as likely to call the sheriff department's direct line and ask for Travis or Gage or one of the other officers by name.

Wade Tomlinson met Travis on the sidewalk in front of their store. "Thanks for stopping by,

Sheriff," he said. He crossed his arms over his beefy chest, the eagle tattoo on his biceps flexing. A vein pulsed in his shaved head. "Though I guess we wasted your time."

"Adelaide said you had a shoplifter?"

"Yeah, but he got away, right after I called." He led the way inside the shop, which smelled of canvas, leather and rope. Climbing rope in every color of the rainbow hung from hooks along the back wall, while everything from stainless-steel coffee mugs to ice axes and crampons filled the shelves.

Wade's business partner, Brock Ryan, looked up from rearranging a display of T-shirts. The one in his hand, Travis noted, bore the legend *Do It In the Outdoors*. "Hey, Travis," he said. "You didn't pass a skinny teenager in a red beanie on your way over here, did you?"

"No," Travis said. "Was that your shoplifter?"

"Yeah. I caught him red-handed shoving a hundred-dollar water filter down his pants. I sat him down up front by the register and told him we would wait until you got here before we decided whether or not to file charges."

Unlike Wade, who was short and stocky, Brock was tall and lean, with the squinting gaze of a man who had spent long hours in the sun and wind.

"What happened after that?" Travis asked.

"I turned my back to get a tray of fishing flies out of the case for a customer and the kid took off," Brock said, his face reddening.

"Did the kid give you a name?" Travis asked. "Did you recognize him?"

Both men shook their heads. "He wasn't from around here," Wade said. "He wouldn't say anything to us, so we figured we'd let you see if you could get anything out of him."

"Maybe you two scared him enough he won't come back," Travis said.

"Burns me up when somebody comes in here and tries to take what we've worked hard for," Brock said. He punched his hand in his fist. "If that kid ever shows his face here again, I'll make sure he never tries to steal from me again."

Travis put a hand on the tall man's shoulder. "Don't let your temper get the best of you," he said. "If the kid comes back, call the office and one of us will take care of it."

Brock hesitated, then nodded. "Right."

A third man emerged from a door at the back of the shop—a lean, broad-shouldered guy in a black knit beanie. He looked as if he had been carved from iron—all sharp angles and hard muscle. He scanned Travis from head to toe, lingering a moment on the badge on his chest, and Travis wouldn't have called his expression friendly. "Do you have a new employee?" Travis asked, nodding toward the man.

Brock glanced over his shoulder. "That's Ian," he said. "A friend of mine."

Ian nodded, but didn't offer to shake hands. "I'll wait in back," he said to Brock, and exited the way he had come.

"Your friend got a problem with cops?" Travis asked.

"He's not comfortable with new people," Wade said. "He did four tours in Iraq and Afghanistan. He has trouble sometimes with PTSD."

Travis nodded. Maybe that explained the hostility he had felt from the guy. Or maybe Travis was more suspicious than most people. A hazard of the job, he supposed. "I doubt you'll have any more trouble from your shoplifter," he said to Wade and Brock. "You probably scared him off. But I'll keep my eyes open."

"Thanks."

Travis returned to his SUV and climbed in. He started the vehicle and was about to pull out of his parking spot when he glanced over at the passenger seat and slammed on the brakes. The box and the rock that had been thrown through Lacy's window were gone.

Chapter Three

"Why would someone steal the rock?" Lacy folded her arms over her chest and took a step back from Travis. He had shown up at her house this morning—supposedly to "check on" her and her family. But then he had come out with this crazy story about someone taking the rock that had been thrown through her window. "Do you think I took it or something?"

"No!" He put up his hands, as if he wanted to reach for her, then put them down. "I wanted you to know because you're the victim in this case, and you have a right to know what's going on."

She unfolded her arms, relaxing a little. She had insisted on talking with him on the front porch—mainly so her parents wouldn't overhear. Her mom and dad meant well, but they tended to hover now that she was back home. "So someone just opened the door of your sheriff's department vehicle and took the evidence box?" she asked. "How does that happen? Wasn't your door locked?"

"No one locks their car doors around here." He looked sheepish—an endearing expression, really—and she didn't want to feel anything like that for him. "Besides, it's a cop car. Who breaks into a cop car? And to steal a rock?"

"Maybe they didn't know what was in the box?" she said. "Or maybe somebody is pranking you—wants to give you a hard time."

"Maybe." He put one booted foot up on a metal footlocker her mom used as a side table on the porch, and she tried not to notice the way the khaki fabric stretched over his muscular thigh. She didn't like being around Travis, but apparently her body couldn't ignore the fact that he was the sexiest guy she'd been near in three years. "Or maybe whoever threw the rock took it because they thought I could use it somehow to link them to the crime," he added.

She forced her mind away from ogling the sheriff's hot body to what was surely a more important matter. "Can you do that?" she asked. "Would a rock have fingerprints on it or something?"

"The surface was too rough to give good latent prints, and it looked like a common enough rock."

"What about DNA?" she asked.

He laughed. "No offense, but no one does DNA testing for an act of vandalism. It's expensive, and the results take a while to come back."

She lowered herself to the cushioned rattan love seat. Her mother had made the cushions out of flowered chintz, faded now by the summer sun, but all the more comfortable and homey for it. "If the person who threw the rock stole it out of your SUV, that means they knew you had it. They must have been watching and seen you come to the house to get it."

Travis sat beside her, the cushion dipping under his weight. She caught the scent of soap and starch and clean man, and fought to keep from leaning toward him. "Maybe," he said. "Or maybe they knew your family would call my office to report the threat, they saw my SUV and decided to take a look inside."

"Either way, I'm completely creeped out." She gripped the edge of the love seat. She had thought when she walked out of prison that she would feel free again, but she still felt trapped. Watched.

"I talked to Brenda Stenson yesterday," Travis said. "She's okay with us going through Andy's files."

Lacy nodded. "I'm not looking forward to that, you know."

"I understand. But I'm hoping coming at the

files cold after a few years away, you'll spot something or remember something that didn't seem relevant before."

"What about the other evidence from the crime scene?" she asked. "Wasn't there anything that pointed to someone besides me as the murderer? Or did you conveniently overlook that?" She didn't even try to keep the sharp edge from her voice.

"I guess I deserved that," Travis said. "But no—there wasn't anything. Wade Tomlinson reported seeing a woman who looked like you near the office shortly before Andy would have died. Obviously, that wasn't you. It might help if we could find this woman, but we don't have much to go on—Wade admitted he only saw her from the back, and only for a few seconds, before she entered the office. I'll question him again, but I doubt he'll have anything useful to add."

"Right. Who remembers anything very clearly that happened three years ago?" Lacy sighed.

"I think Andy's files are the best place for us to start," Travis said.

"Andy hadn't been in practice very long," Lacy said. "Still, he had a couple of big cabinets full of files. Everything was backed up on the computer, too, but he had been trained by a man who liked to keep paper copies of everything, and Andy was the same way. It will take a while to go through everything."

"We can do a couple of boxes at a time. You could even bring them back here to look through."

"Do you trust me to look through them by myself?" she asked.

"It would look better in court if we went through them together," Travis said. "Otherwise, a good defense attorney would point out that you had a strong motive to make people believe someone else murdered Andy. They could suggest you planted evidence in the files."

She fought against her inclination to bristle at what sounded to her ears like an accusation. After all, she knew all too well how attorneys could twist the most mundane events to make someone look guilty to a jury. "I guess you're right," she admitted. She stretched her legs out in front of her. "So how do you want to do this?"

"I'll get together with Brenda this afternoon and go over to the storage unit with her. I'll select a couple of boxes to go through first, seal them in her presence, get her to sign off on them, then bring them here. We'll open them together and start going through the contents.

Maybe I'll even video everything, just in case there's any question."

"You're very thorough."

"I'm determined not to make any mistakes this time."

And I'm determined not to let you, she thought.

ANDY STENSON'S STORAGE unit was located in a long metal shed at the end of Fireline Road on the edge of town. Weedy fields extended beyond the chain-link fence that surrounded the shed on all sides, the land sloping upward from there toward Dakota Ridge and the mountains beyond. With no traffic and no neighbors, the location was peaceful, even beautiful, with the first summer wildflowers blooming in the fields and a china blue sky arching overhead. But there wasn't anything beautiful about Travis's errand here today.

Brenda agreed to meet him, and when he pulled into the rutted drive, he found her waiting at the far end, key in hand. "You open it," she said, pushing the key at him. "I haven't been in here since before Andy died. I paid a cleaning company to move all his stuff out here."

"Are you okay being here now?" Travis asked, studying her face. Tension lines fanned out from her mouth, but she didn't look on the verge of a breakdown.

"I'm okay," she said. "I just want to get this over with."

He unfastened the padlock and rolled up the metal door of the unit. Sunlight illuminated jumbled stacks of file boxes. Furniture filled one corner of the unit—several filing cabinets and some chairs and Andy's desk, scarred and dusty. The chair he had been sitting in when he died, stained with his blood, was in a police storage unit, logged as evidence.

Brenda traced a finger across the dust on the desktop. Was she thinking about her young husband, who had been taken from her when they were still practically newlyweds? She squared her shoulders and turned to study the file boxes. "There's a lot of stuff here," she said. "Do you know what you want?"

"I want to look at his case files." Travis studied the labels on the boxes, then removed the lid from one with the notation Clients, A through C. "I know you said you didn't know much about his work, but who would you say was his biggest client at the time he died?"

"That one's easy enough. Hake Development." She pointed to a box on the bottom of the pile, with the single word *HAKE* scrawled on the end. "Andy couldn't believe his luck when Henry Hake hired him instead of one of the big-city firms. Mr. Hake said he wanted to support local business." She chuckled. "He did that, all right. Hake Development accounted for a big percentage of Andy's income that year." Her voice trailed away at these last words, as if she was remembering once more the reason the good fortune had ended.

"All right, I'll start with this one." Travis moved aside the stack of boxes to retrieve the Hake files, and found a second box, also marked Hake, behind it.

He set the boxes on the desk, then went to his car and retrieved the evidence tape and seals. "You're verifying that I haven't opened the boxes or tampered with them in any way," he said.

"I am." He ran a strip of wide tape horizontally and vertically across each box, sealing the tops in place, then asked Brenda to write her name across each piece of tape.

"I'll video opening the boxes," he said. "With Lacy's parents as witnesses. That ought to satisfy any court that we aren't up to anything underhanded."

Brenda watched him, arms folded across her chest. "I hope you find something useful in there," she said. "Though I can't imagine what."

"What was Andy doing for Hake, do you know?" Travis asked.

"Just the legal paperwork for the mining claims Henry Hake had bought and planned to develop as a vacation resort. It wouldn't have been a big deal, except that environmental group got an injunction against the development and Andy was fighting that."

"I remember a little about that," Travis said. "They had a Ute Indian chief speak at a council meeting or something like that?"

"He wasn't a chief, just a tribal representative—a friend of Paige Riddell's. She was president of the group, I believe."

"Maybe someone who didn't want the development thought taking out Hake's lawyer would stop the threat of the injunction being overturned," Travis said.

"If they thought that, they were wrong. Hake hired another firm to represent him—someone out of Denver this time. I don't know what happened after that, though I guess he hasn't done anything with the property yet."

"Wouldn't hurt to check it out," Travis said.

He picked up the first box as his phone beeped. Setting it down, he answered the call. "A car just crashed through the front window of the Cake Walk Café." Adelaide sounded out of breath with excitement. "Gage is headed there.

Dwight and Roberta are in training today. I can call someone from another shift in if you want me to. The ambulance is en route from Junction."

"I'll handle it. I'm on my way." Travis hung up the phone and studied the boxes. He could take them with him, but after what happened yesterday, he didn't want to risk someone trying to get hold of them. He returned the keys to Brenda. "Lock up after I've left. I'll have to send someone to retrieve these later."

"Is everything okay?" she asked.

"Apparently, someone crashed into the café."

Brenda covered her mouth with her hand. "I hope no one was hurt."

"Me, too."

In the car, he called Lacy. "I picked out two boxes of files from Andy's storage and got them sealed, but now I have to go on a call. It will be a while before I can get back to them."

"I can pick them up," she said. "If they're already sealed, it shouldn't make any difference, should it?"

He debated as he guided his SUV down the rutted dirt road leading away from the storage facility. "Ride out here with Brenda and have her deliver you and the boxes back to your house." Before she could protest, he added, "It's not that I don't trust you, but I don't want to give any lawyers the opportunity to object."

"All right. I'd like to visit with Brenda, anyway."

"I'll get back with you to set a time for the two of us to get together," he said, and ended the call. As much as he wanted to find the person who had killed Andy Stenson, his job wouldn't allow him to focus all his attention on one case. Right now he had a mess to clean up at the café.

LACY ENDED THE call from Travis and looked out the front window. The glass company had been out this morning to replace the broken pane and she had a clear view of the street. The car she had noticed earlier was still there—a faded blue sedan that had been parked in front of a vacation cottage three doors down and across the street from her parents' house. The cottage had a For Sale sign in front, but Lacy was pretty sure no potential buyer had been inside the cottage all this time.

She retrieved her mother's bird-watching binoculars from the bookcase by the door and returned to the window, training the glasses on the car. A man sat behind the wheel, head bent, attention on the phone in his hand. He was middle-aged, with light brown hair and narrow shoulders. He didn't look particularly threatening, but then again, looks could be deceiving. And it wasn't as if it would have taken that much brawn to throw that rock through the window yesterday afternoon.

She shifted the binoculars to the license plate on the car. BRH575. She'd remember the number and think about asking Travis to check it out. He owed her more than a few favors, didn't he? She had almost mentioned the car to him while they were talking just now, but she didn't want to give him the idea that she needed him for anything. She didn't like to think of herself as hardened, but three years in prison had taught her to look out for herself.

She brought the glasses up to the man in the car and gasped as it registered that he had raised his own pair of binoculars and was focused on her. She took two steps back, fairly certain that he couldn't see her inside the house, but unwilling to take chances. What was he doing out there, watching the house? Watching *her*? She replaced the binoculars on the shelf and headed toward the back of the house. As she passed her mother's home office, Jeanette looked up from her computer. A former teacher, she now worked as an online tutor. "Who was that on the phone?" she asked.

Lacy started to lie, but couldn't think of one

that sounded convincing enough. "Travis canceled our meeting to go over Andy's files," she said. "He had to go on a call."

"I hope everything's all right." Jeanette swiveled her chair around to face her daughter. "You're okay, working with Travis?" she asked. "I know you don't have the warmest feelings toward him, and I'll admit, I had my doubts, too. But when I saw how hard he worked to clear your name…" She compressed her lips, struggling for control. "I really don't think you'd be standing here right now if it wasn't for him."

"I wouldn't have been in prison in the first place if it wasn't for him, either," Lacy said.

Jeanette said nothing, merely gave Lacy a pleading look.

"I'm okay working with him," Lacy said. "I don't know how much good going through those old files will do, but I'm willing to help." She turned away again.

"Where are you going?" her mother asked.

"I thought I'd take a walk."

"That's nice."

Lacy didn't wait for more, but hurried toward the back door. All the houses on this street backed up to the river, and a public trail ran along the bank. She let herself out the back gate and followed this trail up past four houses, then slipped alongside the fourth house, crossed the street behind the blue sedan, and walked up to the passenger side of the vehicle. The driver had lowered the front windows a few inches, so Lacy leaned in and said, loudly, "What do you think you're doing, spying on me?"

The man juggled his phone, then dropped it. "You—you startled me!" he gasped.

"I saw you watching me," Lacy said. "I want to know why."

"I didn't want to intrude. I was merely trying to get a feel for the neighborhood, and see how you were doing."

"Who are you, and why do you care how I'm doing?" She was getting more annoyed with this guy by the second.

"I'm sorry. I should have introduced myself. Alvin Exeter. I'm a writer. I specialize in true-crime stories." He leaned across the seat and extended his hand toward her.

She ignored the outstretched hand. "I didn't commit a crime," she said. "Or don't you read the papers?"

"No, of course. And that's what I want to write about," he said. "I'm planning a book on your wrongful conviction and its aftermath."

"And you were planning to write about me without telling me?"

"No, no, of course not. I would love to interview you for the book, get your side of the story. I was merely looking for the right opportunity to approach you."

"Get lost, Mr. Exeter," she said. "And if you try to write about me, I'll sue."

"You could try," he said. "But you're a public figure now. I have every right to tell your story, based on court documents, news articles and interviews with anyone associated with you. Though, of course, the story will be more complete if you agree to cooperate with me."

"No one I know will talk to you," she said. Though how could she be sure of that, really?

"That's not true. Sheriff Travis Walker has already agreed to speak with me."

"Travis is going to talk to you about my case?"

"We have an appointment in a couple days." Alvin leaned back in his seat, relaxed. "What do you think the public will make of the man who sent you to prison speaking, while you remain silent?"

"I think you can both go to hell," she said, and turned and walked away. She could feel his eyes on her all the way back to the house, but she wouldn't give him the satisfaction of seeing her turn around. She marched onto the porch and yanked at the door—but of course it was locked, and she didn't have her key. She had to ring the doorbell and wait for her mother to answer.

"Lacy, where is your key?" Jeanette asked as she followed Lacy into the house.

"I forgot and left it in my room." Lacy stalked into the kitchen and filled a glass of water.

"What's wrong?" Jeanette asked. "You look all flushed. Did something happen to upset you?"

"I'll be fine, Mother." She would be fine as soon as she talked to Travis, and told him what he could do with Andy's client files. Travis Walker was the last person she would ever help with anything.

Chapter Four

Travis waited while Tammy Patterson snapped another photo of the red Camry with its nose buried in the pile of crumbling brick that had once been the front wall of the Cake Walk Café. She stepped back and gave him a grateful smile. "Thanks, Sheriff. This is going to look great on the front page of the next issue."

"I'll want a copy of those pictures for my insurance company." Iris Desmet, owner of the Cake Walk, joined Tammy and Travis on the sidewalk.

"Sure thing, Ms. Desmet," Tammy said. "And I'm really sorry about the café. I didn't mean to sound like this accident was good news or anything."

"I know you didn't, dear." Iris patted Tammy's shoulder. "I'm just relieved no one was hurt. It was our slow time of day and I didn't have anyone sitting up front."

Tammy pulled out her notebook and began

scribbling away. Twenty-three but looking about fifteen, Tammy was working her very first job out of college for the tiny *Eagle Mountain Examiner*. What she lacked in experience, she made up for in enthusiasm. "The paramedic told me they think the driver of the car is going to be okay, too. They think he had some kind of episode with his blood sugar."

"Better confirm that with the hospital before you go printing it," Travis said.

"Oh, yes, sir. I sure will." She flashed another smile and hurried away, no doubt thrilled to have something more exciting to write about than the town council's budget meeting or the school board's decision to remove soda machines from the lunchroom.

Iris moved closer to Travis. "Do you think the guy will lose his license over this?" she asked, nodding toward the pile of rubble.

"I don't know," Travis said. "Maybe. Either way, he's probably going to have trouble finding someone to insure him."

"I hope he's got good insurance," Iris said.

"I guess you'll have to close the café for a while, to remodel," Travis said.

"I imagine so. Then again, I've been thinking how nice it would be to visit my sister for a few days. She and her husband live up on

Lake Coeur d'Alene, in Idaho. Pretty country up there. Still, it'll be hard on my employees."

"I'll keep my ears open, let you know if I hear of anyone looking for short-term help, until you can get open again."

"Thanks, Sheriff." She looked him up and down. "And how are you doing?"

"I'm fine."

"I guess it's a load off your mind, with Lacy Milligan being home again, out of prison."

"I'm glad she's home," he said, cautious.

"But now you're back to the question you started with—who killed Andy Stenson?"

"I'm working on that," he said. "Do you have any ideas?"

"No. But I've been thinking, the way you do when you live alone and wake up in the middle of the night and can't sleep. I've always wondered about that woman."

"What woman?" Travis asked.

"The dark-haired one Wade testified he saw going into Andy's office shortly before Andy was killed," Iris said. "If it wasn't Lacy—and I guess it wasn't, since she was at that basketball game—but if it wasn't her, who was it?"

"Maybe it was Andy's killer," Travis said. "Or someone who saw the killer. But again—we don't know who it was. Do you have any ideas?"

"Maybe look for a client of Andy's who fits

that description?" Iris shook her head. "I know I'm not helping, I just like to think about these things."

"Well, if you think of anything else, let me know," Travis said.

He walked back to his SUV and drove to the office. Adelaide rose to meet him. "Sheriff—"

"Not now, Adelaide," he said. "I'm not in the mood to talk."

"But, Sheriff—"

He walked past her, into his office, and collided with Lacy Milligan.

As collisions went, this one was more pleasurable than most, he thought, as he wrapped his arms around Lacy to steady them both. She squirmed against him, giving him plenty of opportunity to enjoy the sensation of her soft curves sliding against him. But he wasn't the kind to take advantage of the situation. As soon as he was certain neither of them was going to fall, he released his hold on her. "What can I do for you, Lacy?" he asked.

"Do for me? You've done enough for me," she said, voice rising along with the flush of pink to her cheeks. "I want you to stop. I want you to leave me alone."

Aware of Adelaide's sharp ears attuned to every word, Travis reached back and shut the door to his office. "Let's sit down and you can tell me what this is about. Is there something specific I've done that has you so upset?"

He lowered himself into the chair behind his desk, but she remained mobile, prowling the small office like a caged animal. "Alvin Exeter," she said. "How could you even think of talking to that man about me?"

Travis squinted, thinking. "Who is Alvin Exeter?"

"He's a horrible man who says he's writing a book about me—about what happened to me. He said he has an appointment to talk with you."

Travis picked up his phone and pressed the button to ring Adelaide. She picked up right away and he put her on speaker. "Do you want me to bring in coffee for you and your guest?" she asked.

"No. Do I have an appointment with someone named Alvin Exeter tomorrow?"

"Two days from now, 9:30 a.m."

"So you asked me if I wanted to talk to this Exeter guy and I said yes?"

He could picture her scowl as she assumed her chilliest schoolmarm tone. "I didn't have to ask you. You have a stated open-door policy for citizens who want to speak to you."

So he did. "What does he want to talk to me about?" Travis asked.

"He said he's writing a human interest story on rural law enforcement."

"Thanks." Travis hung up the phone and looked at Lacy. "Did you get all that?"

"You really didn't know you had an appointment with him?"

"No." Which perhaps made him look like a poor manager in her eyes, but better than looking like a traitor. "And, apparently, Adelaide didn't know the real reason behind the appointment. He lied about his purpose in wanting to see me."

"Are you still going to talk to him?"

"Only to tell him to leave you alone. That's really all I can do. I can't keep him from approaching other people and asking them questions. Though if he bothers you again, I can arrest him for harassment."

She dropped into a chair and glared at him. The memory of her warmth still clung to him, making him conscious of the short distance between them, of how beautiful and prickly and vulnerable she was—and how mixed up and charged his feelings for her were.

"You really are making this difficult, you know?" she said.

"Making what difficult?"

"For me to hate you. I spent the last three years building you up in my mind as this horrible monster and now that you're here, in front of me, you insist on being so...so decent!"

He told himself he wouldn't laugh. He wouldn't even smile. "If anyone bothers you— Exeter or anyone else—let me know," he said. "I've got your back."

"I don't need you to be my bodyguard," she said.

"My job is to protect the citizens of this county, and you're one of them."

"So that's what I am to you, then? Your job?"

"No." She was his biggest regret. His responsibility, even. He'd helped ruin her life and now he felt obligated to help her put it back together. If she had asked he would have found her a job or given her money, but she wouldn't ask for those things—she wouldn't take them if he offered. But he could do everything in his power to protect her—to shield her from the aftereffects of the damage he'd done to her. He couldn't tell her any of that, so instead, he tapped the badge on his chest. "You're someone I hurt and I want to make that up to you, but mostly, I want to make sure you aren't hurt again."

She looked away, cheeks still flushed, then shoved out of the chair. "I'd better go. I... I'll look at those files whenever you're ready."

"Iris Desmet over at the Cake Walk said

something interesting to me this afternoon," Travis said. "She said we should look for any client of Andy's who matched the description Wade Tomlinson gave of the woman whom he saw at Andy's office about the time Andy would have been killed."

"I don't remember any clients who looked like me," she said.

"Think about it. Maybe a name will come to you."

"So that's your new theory about who killed Andy—this mysterious woman?"

"Not necessarily. But if she was around near the time when Andy was killed, maybe she saw something or remembers something." He frowned. "I should have followed up on that when Wade first mentioned her."

"But you didn't, because you thought he was talking about me," she said.

"That was a mistake. A big one on my part." One he wouldn't make again.

She turned to leave. "Let me know how it goes with Alvin Exeter," she said. "I'm curious to know what he has to say."

He walked her to the door. Even with her bad prison haircut and too-pale skin she was beautiful. The kind of woman a lot of men might underestimate, but not him. He would never underestimate Lacy Milligan again.

"IT'S SO GOOD to see you." Brenda greeted Lacy on the front porch of the Milligans' house the next morning with these words and a hug that surprised her with its fierceness. When Brenda pulled away, her eyes glinted with unshed tears. "I'm sorrier than you can know that I didn't contact you while you were in prison," she said. "I started to write more than once, but I just couldn't think what to say."

"I wouldn't have known what to say, either," Lacy said. After all, she had been convicted of murdering Brenda's husband. That went far beyond merely awkward. "I'm just really glad you don't have any hard feelings now."

"I'm thrilled you're home," Brenda said. "I could never accept that you had anything to do with Andy's death. When Travis told me he had found evidence that proved you were innocent, I was so relieved."

"Even though it means the real killer is still out there?" Lacy asked.

"I didn't think of that until later."

"So Travis told you he was going to try to free me?" Lacy asked.

"He told me before he told the press. He wanted to make sure I was prepared." Brenda touched Lacy's arm. "He told me you still have bad feelings toward him, and I don't blame you.

But he really is a good man—one of the best men I know."

Lacy nodded. She might not be ready to forgive Travis Walker for stealing three years of her life, but she was woman enough to see the good in him, in spite of his mistakes. "I guess he told you why we're looking through Andy's files," she said.

"Yes. I don't think you'll find anything useful, but I guess we can hope." She pulled her keys from her purse. "Are you ready to go get the boxes? I would have swung by the storage unit and picked them up myself, but Travis said it was better to do things this way."

"After the mistakes he made at my trial, I guess he's being extra cautious," Lacy said.

"I can't help but hope that this time he finds the real murderer," Brenda said. "I think it would help all of us put this behind us." She climbed into the driver's seat of her car, while Lacy slid into the passenger seat.

"I do want to put this behind me," Lacy said. "I'm still adjusting to the idea that I'm really free."

"Do you think you'll stay in Eagle Mountain?" Brenda asked.

"I don't know," Lacy said. "This is my home, but even in three years, things have changed."

"Not that much, surely," Brenda said. She turned the car onto Main.

"There are new houses, new businesses, new people I don't know. We even have a new mayor." Lacy gestured toward the banner that hung over the street. "And what's this Pioneer Days Festival?" she asked. "That wasn't around when I left."

"It's a whole weekend of events celebrating local history," Brenda said. "Jan came up with the idea when she was mayor and it's really been a boon for the town coffers." Jan Selkirk had been mayor when Lacy had left town, and, after leaving office, had taken over management of the history museum where Brenda worked.

"I guess I remember some talk about a local celebration to commemorate the town's founding," Lacy said. "I didn't think it would be such a big deal."

"I guess it morphed over time into a really big deal," Brenda said. "Tourists come and stay all weekend. All the local motels and inns are sold out, and we have all kinds of special events at the museum."

"Sounds like fun." Lacy swiveled in her seat as they passed a pile of wreckage. "What happened to the Cake Walk?" she asked.

"You didn't hear?" Brenda slowed as they

passed the rubble, which was cordoned off with orange tape. "That was why Travis had to leave without picking up the file boxes. A guy ran his car right into it yesterday afternoon. Jan told me she heard the poor man had a stroke. They ended up taking him to the hospital. Fortunately, no one inside was hurt."

"I was at the sheriff's office yesterday afternoon and Travis never said a word about it," Lacy said.

"Oh? Why were you at the sheriff's office?" Brenda didn't try to hide her curiosity.

Lacy leaned back in the seat and sighed. "There's a man in town who says he's writing a book about me. I complained to Travis about him." No point in going into her accusations that Travis was selling her out to this writer.

"Oh, dear. I suppose that was bound to happen," Brenda said.

"I'm surprised he hasn't gotten in touch with you yet."

"When he does, I'll tell him what he can do with his book project," Brenda said.

"He said he was going to write about me, whether I cooperate or not. I guess I'll have to get used to that kind of thing. He said I was a public figure now."

"Oh, Lacy." Brenda reached over and rubbed her arm. "I'm sorry."

Lacy straightened and forced a smile onto her lips. "It'll be okay. What's one lousy book in the scheme of things?"

For the next twenty minutes, the two friends discussed the Pioneer Days Festival, new businesses that had moved to town in Lacy's absence and a new television series they were both watching. By the time they reached the storage facility, they had relaxed into the easy banter of old friends.

"I remember this place," Lacy said as she climbed out of the car at the storage unit. "I used to give Andy a hard time about it being so far out here on the edge of town."

"I guess nobody really wants a place like this in their backyard," Brenda said. "Plus, the land is cheaper out here." She undid the lock and pulled up the door.

The first thing Lacy spotted was a Victorian lamp that had sat on her desk in the front office of Andy Stenson's law practice. Seeing it now, shade crooked and grayed with dust, gave her a jolt. Her gaze shifted to the big walnut desk where Andy had sat. It had usually been covered in papers, but she recognized the lovely dark finish. So odd to see these familiar things out of context.

"After Andy died, I was such a wreck," Brenda said, as if reading Lacy's mind. "I hired a couple of guys to clean out the office and put everything here. I hadn't even looked at any of it until I was out here with Travis yesterday."

"There was no reason you should have had to look at it," Lacy said. "I hope Travis is right, and we find something useful in all these papers."

"These are the two boxes he wants to start with." Brenda pointed to two white file boxes, their tops crisscrossed with red and white tape. "All the files for Hake Development."

"I was surprised when my mom told me Mr. Hake still hasn't done anything with that property," Lacy said. "I remember he had big plans for a bunch of luxury homes—even a golf course."

"An environmental group successfully got an injunction to delay construction," Brenda said. "I'm not sure what's going on with it now. Maybe Henry Hake changed his mind."

"Maybe." Lacy picked up one box, while Brenda carried the other to the car. Boxes safely in the back seat, Brenda locked up again and the two friends set out once more.

"They haven't done much to fix this road," Lacy said as they bumped over a series of ruts on the gravel track that led away from the storage units.

"I guess with no one living out this way, it's not a priority," Brenda said.

"Right." Lacy looked over her shoulder to make sure the file boxes hadn't slid off the seat, and was surprised to see a pickup truck following them. "If no one lives out here, I wonder who that is?" she asked.

Brenda glanced in the rearview mirror. "I don't recognize the truck," she said.

"Maybe it's a tourist," Lacy said. "He could be looking for somewhere to hike. Or maybe it's someone else with a storage unit."

"It looks like a ranch truck, with that brush guard on the front." The heavy pipe, gate-like structure attached to the front bumper would protect the headlights and grill from being damaged by brush when a rancher drove through the fields.

"I didn't see any other vehicles there," Lacy said. "And we didn't pass anyone on our way out here."

"Whoever he is, he's driving way too fast for this road," Brenda said.

Lacy glanced over her shoulder again. The truck was gaining on them, a great plume of dust rising up in its wake. "He's going to have to slow down," she said. "Or run us off the road."

Even as she spoke, the truck zoomed up, its

front bumper almost touching the rear bumper of Brenda's car. The lone occupant wore a ball cap pulled low on his forehead, a black bandanna tied over his mouth and nose.

"What does he think he's doing?" Brenda's voice rose in alarm. The car lurched as she tapped the brakes and Lacy grabbed on to the door for support. The screech of metal on metal filled the vehicle, which jolted again as the bumpers connected.

Brenda cursed, and struggled to hold on to the wheel. Lacy wrenched around to stare at the driver once more, but she could make out nothing of his face. He backed off and she sagged back into her seat once more.

"He's crazy," Brenda said. The car sped up, bumping along the rough road. "As soon as I can, I'm going to pull over and let him pa—"

She never finished the sentence, as the truck slammed into them once again, sending them skidding off the road and rolling down the embankment.

Chapter Five

"All units report to Fireline Road for a vehic-ular accident with possible injuries." The dis-patcher's voice sounded clear on the otherwise quiet radio. Travis, on his way to lunch, hit the button to respond. "Unit one headed to Fireline Road," he said. He switched on his siren and headed out, falling in behind Gage, an ambu-lance bringing up the rear of their little parade.

As he drove, he checked the GPS location the dispatcher had sent over. The accident looked to have occurred about two miles this side of the storage units, an area with a sharp curve and a steep drop-off. He slowed as the screen on his dash indicated they were nearing the site. Gage pulled to the side of the road and Travis parked behind him. He joined his brother on the rough shoulder, and stared down at a white Subaru Outback, resting on its side on the steep slope, wedged against a solitary lodgepole pine tree.

Gage raised binoculars to his eyes. "Looks

like there's at least one person in there—maybe two," he said.

Two EMTs joined them—a freckle-faced young guy Travis didn't know, and Emmet Baxter, a rescue service veteran. "OnStar called it in," Baxter said, nodding to the wrecked Subaru. "They tried to contact the driver but no one responded. Since the airbags had deployed, it triggered an automatic call."

"I'll call in the plate," Gage said. "See if we can get a possible ID on the driver."

"Go ahead, but I know who it is," Travis said, the tightness in his chest making it difficult to take a full breath. "That's Brenda Stenson's car. And the passenger is probably Lacy Milligan. The two of them were supposed to drive out here to pick up some of Andy Stenson's files from storage." He pulled out his phone and punched in Brenda's number. It rang five times before going to voice mail. He got the same results with Lacy's number. He swore and stuffed the phone back in the case on his hip, then stepped down off the edge of the road.

Gage grabbed his arm and pulled him back. "Where do you think you're going?"

"I'm going down to them. They could be hurt."

"Yeah, and one wrong move could send the

vehicle the rest of the way down the slope and you with it," Gage said.

Travis studied the car and realized Gage was right. "Get Search and Rescue out here. And a wrecker. We'll have to stabilize the car, then get the women out."

Gage made the call and then there was nothing to do but wait. Travis walked the roadside, studying the surface for clues to what had happened. Soon, Gage joined him. "You can see the skid marks where they went off here," Travis said, pointing to the long tracks in the gravel.

"Doesn't really look like an overcorrection, or like she was going too fast and missed the curve," Gage said.

Travis shook his head. "Brenda's not that kind of driver. Anyway, look at this." He pointed to another set of skid marks behind the first, these veering away from the edge of the road.

"Another vehicle?" Gage asked.

"Yeah." Travis walked a little farther and squatted down at a place where broken glass glittered amid the gravel in the road. "This is probably where it struck her car—broke the rear headlights." He glanced back as the first of the Search and Rescue team arrived.

"Accident or deliberate?" Gage asked.

"They left the scene. That's a crime, even if the collision itself was an accident. But this feels deliberate to me. The weather's good, light's good. No way a person traveling behind Brenda's car wouldn't have seen her."

"Maybe the other driver's brakes failed?"

Travis straightened. "How often does that really happen?"

He and Gage walked back to meet the SAR volunteers. Travis was relieved to see an orthopedic doctor who worked weekends at the emergency clinic in Gunnison, as well as a local mountain guide, Jacob Zander. "You remember Dr. Pete, right?" Jacob said.

The men shook hands, then turned their attention to the wrecked car. "We've got two women in the vehicle," Travis said. "We don't know how badly they're hurt, but they didn't respond to OnStar."

"We need to secure the vehicle before we can do anything," Dr. Pete said.

Another carload of SAR volunteers pulled onto the shoulder, followed by a flatbed wrecker with a driver and passenger. The wrecker driver climbed out and shambled over to join them.

"Got a challenge for you," Gage said, nodding to the wedged car.

The driver, whose jacket identified him

as Bud, considered the scene below, then shrugged. "I've seen worse."

"Can you secure the vehicle so that the EMTs can get down to take care of the driver and passenger?" Travis asked.

"I'll take care of it." He returned to the wrecker and his passenger—who turned out to be a woman with curly brown hair—climbed out. They conferred for a moment, then both started climbing down the slope, draped in ropes and chains. Dr. Pete and Jacob followed.

"What should we do now?" Gage asked.

Travis leaned back against his SUV, arms crossed, eyes fixed on the scene below. "We wait," he said. And pray that his search for whoever had run Brenda and Lacy off the road didn't turn into a hunt for a killer.

LACY WOKE TO pain in her head, and the taste of blood in her mouth. She moaned and forced herself to open her eyes against the searing pain. "What's happening?" she asked.

The words came out garbled, and her mouth hurt.

"Don't try to talk, ma'am. You were in an accident."

"An accident?" She blinked, and the face of the man who was speaking came into focus. He was blond, with freckles and glasses.

"It looks like you hit your head," he said. "Can you tell me if it hurts anywhere else?"

"No... I don't know."

The man leaned in through the passenger-side window, which was broken. He shined a light into her eyes and she moaned again and turned her head away. When she opened her eyes, she stared at Brenda, who lay in the driver's seat, mouth slack, white powder covering her face and shoulders. "Brenda!" Lacy tried to lean toward her.

"We're taking care of your friend. We need you to stay calm." Her rescuer reached around behind her. "I'm going to put this brace on your neck," he said. "It's just a precaution. What's your name?"

"Lacy. Lacy Milligan." The brace felt stiff and awkward, and smelled of disinfectant. Her head felt clearer now—she was remembering what had happened. But with memory came fear. "Where is the truck that ran us off the road?" she asked.

"I don't know about any truck." She heard the ripping sound of a hook and loop tape being pulled apart and repositioned. "My name is Pete. I'm a doctor."

Then a second man was leaning in beside Pete. "Lacy, it's Travis. How are you doing?"

"My head hurts." She closed her eyes again.

"Stay with us, Lacy," Dr. Pete said. "Open your eyes for me."

"Tell me about the truck, Lacy," Travis said.

She struggled to do as they asked, fighting against a wave of nausea and extreme fatigue. "The truck was black," she said. "With one of those big things on the front—iron pipe welded to the front bumper."

"A brush guard?" Travis asked.

"Yes. One of those. And it came up behind us really fast. It just—shoved us and we went over." Her heart raced, and she fought to draw a deep breath as panic squeezed her chest. "Is Brenda going to be all right?"

"We're looking after Brenda," Dr. Pete said. "Try not to get upset."

"Do you remember anything else about this truck?" Travis asked. "Did you see the driver? Was there a passenger?"

"No. I mean, I don't know. The windows were so dark I couldn't see much of anything. I think he was wearing a ball cap. And a bandanna tied over his face—like a bank robber in a B movie. It all happened so fast." She tried to shake her head and pain exploded through her with a burst of light behind her eyes. She groaned.

"Do you remember anything about the license plate?" Travis's voice cut through the fog that was trying to overwhelm her. "Or what kind of truck it was?"

"I'm sorry, no."

"Okay, everybody get back, we're going to open this door." The voice came from beyond Lacy's field of vision. Travis and the doctor moved away. A deafening screech rent the air and the car rocked and slipped to the side. Lacy let out a cry and grabbed at nothing. Then the door was wrenched off the driver's side and two men rushed forward. One worked to cut away the steering wheel while two others slashed the seat belt and carefully moved Brenda onto a stretcher. Moments later, someone leaned in the passenger-side window and began sawing at Lacy's seat belt with a blade.

After that, things happened very quickly. A man helped Lacy move into the driver's seat, then she, too, was lifted onto a stretcher. As they strapped her in, Travis leaned over her, his eyes boring into hers. "I'm going to find who did this," he said.

Tears blurred her eyes. "My parents…"

"I'm going there now, to tell them in person and take them to the hospital," he said. "We'll meet you there."

And then he was gone, and all she could see was blue sky, as a group of people she didn't even know worked to carry her to help.

She told herself she was safe now. She was surrounded by people who would help her. But fear still made a cold fist in the middle of her stomach, and she couldn't shake the memory of the impact of that truck on Brenda's car, and the feeling of falling down the mountainside, knowing it was because someone wanted her dead.

TRAVIS PACED THE hallway outside Lacy's room, phone pressed tightly to his ear, shutting out the intercom summons for doctors to report to the emergency room and the rattle of carts as nurses traveled between rooms. "Tell me you've found something," he said when Gage answered the phone.

"I put out the APB like you asked," Gage said. "But we don't have much to go on. There are probably a hundred black trucks in this county alone, and a lot of them are beat-up old ranch trucks. You wouldn't be able to tell at a glance if any of the dents were new or had been there for ten years."

"There was only one black truck that was out on Fireline Road this afternoon," Travis said.

"Face it, Trav, that truck could be in New Mexico by now," Gage said. "Without more to go on, it's going to take a massive stroke of luck to find it."

"Yeah, and nothing about this whole investigation has been lucky. Did you at least get the files out of Brenda's car?" he asked.

"I picked them up myself," Gage said. "They'd been thrown around a bunch in the crash, but that tape you put on the lids actually held pretty well. One of them is kind of split on one side, but everything is in there. I put them on your desk."

"Lock the door to my office and leave it locked until I get there," Travis said.

"You think the guy who ran Brenda and Lacy off the road was after something in those files?" Gage asked.

"I don't know," Travis said. "But we can't afford to overlook anything."

"How are Brenda and Lacy?" Gage asked.

"Lacy has a concussion and a bunch of bruises," Travis said. "They're keeping her overnight for observation, but she should be able to go home with her parents tomorrow. Brenda regained consciousness briefly on the ambulance ride over, but has been drifting in and out ever since. Her head injury is worse, and she had three broken ribs and a punctured lung. They're keeping her in ICU."

"Are Lacy's folks there with her?" Gage asked.

"Yes." They had followed him to the hospital in their car. He had run lights and sirens the whole way, clearing the route, but when they arrived it was clear Jeanette Milligan had been crying, and George was as pale as paper. "They're understandably upset and afraid."

A woman in light blue scrubs came around the corner. "Are you Travis?" she asked.

Travis looked up. "Yes?"

"Ms. Milligan is asking for you."

"Got to go," Travis said, and ended the call.

Mr. and Mrs. Milligan stood on the far side of Lacy's hospital bed when Travis entered the room. Lacy wore a dark pink hospital gown, the black thread from a row of stitches just to the left of her right temple standing out against her pale skin. Both her eyes had begun to blacken, and her upper lip was swollen. Travis must not have done a good job of hiding his shock at her appearance, because she gave him a crooked smile. "They won't let me look in the mirror, but Dad says I look like I lost a boxing match," she said.

"Maybe if anyone asks, that's what you should tell them," Travis said. He moved closer and wrapped both hands around the bed rail, wishing instead that he could hold her hand. But she probably wouldn't welcome the gesture and it wouldn't be the most professional behavior for the county sheriff. Someone had placed a vase of flowers on the bedside table and the peppery-sweet scent of carnations cut through the antiseptic smell.

"Have you found out anything more about the person or people who did this?" Lacy's father asked.

"George." Jeanette gripped her husband's arm.

"It's all right, Mom," Lacy said. "I want to know, too."

All three looked at Travis. "We don't have anything yet," he said. "If you think of anything else that could help us, let me know."

"I'm sorry, no." She shook her head. "Brenda and I went to the storage units and picked up the two boxes you had marked. There wasn't anyone else around while we were there. I mean, there weren't any other vehicles, and it's not that big a place."

"Maybe they parked behind the storage sheds in the back. A truck could probably hide back there."

"Maybe," Lacy said. "It's not like we were looking around for anyone. But they would have had to have been there before we arrived. You can see the gate from the storage unit. That's the only way in, and you have to stop and enter a code to open it."

"It's bad luck no one else was out there who might have seen the guy who hit you," Travis said. "There aren't any houses out that direction, either. We're putting a plea out on the local radio station, and it will be in tomorrow's paper, asking anyone with any information to come forward. Maybe we'll get lucky and someone will know something useful."

"Why would someone do this?" Jeanette asked. "Why would anyone want to hurt Brenda or Lacy? Or was it just a madman, wanting to cause a wreck for kicks?"

"We don't know," Travis said.

"Do you think this is related to the rock that was thrown through our window?" George asked. "Maybe the same person? One of Andy's friends or relatives who still blames Lacy for his murder."

"I'll look into that angle," Travis said. "Though Brenda is the only relative of Andy's I've ever met. I don't remember any parents or siblings attending the trial."

"He was an only child," Lacy said. "His father was dead and his mother had remarried and lives in Hawaii. He didn't see her much. I don't think they were close."

"Still, I'll check and see what I can find," Travis said. "Maybe it was random, or maybe it was related to something else."

"The files!" Lacy put a hand to her mouth. "I just remembered. What happened to the files?"

"Gage got them out of Brenda's car and they're safe for now. Don't worry about them."

"Have you seen Brenda?" Lacy asked. "They told me she's in ICU?"

"I saw her for a few minutes," Travis said. "She's going to be okay, it's just going to take her a little longer. Her head injury was more severe, and she broke some ribs."

"I hope they're giving her good pain meds," Lacy said. "I feel as if, well, as if I was run over by a truck." She gave a small, hysterical laugh.

Her mother squeezed her arm. "You're getting tired," she said. "You need to rest."

"I'll go now," Travis said.

"Please let us know what you find out," Jeanette said. "We're anxious to put this all behind us."

"I will."

He was walking down the hall and was surprised to see Wade Tomlinson walking toward him. "I heard about the accident," Wade said. "I came to see if I could give blood or do anything else to help." He extended his arm to show the bandage wrapped around the crook of his elbow. "They said they didn't need it for Brenda or Lacy, but they could always use donations, and as long as I was here…" He shrugged.

"That was good of you," Travis said. "I was

just in to see Lacy. She's pretty banged up, but she'll be okay. Her parents are with her now."

Wade nodded. "That's good. I hear Brenda is in ICU. Do you know what happened? I mean, the weather was good today, and Brenda doesn't strike me as the type to drive too fast on these mountain roads. Or maybe a deer ran out in front of her and she swerved or something."

Travis debated how much he should say about the accident. Then again, by the time the wrecker driver and the EMTs and the SAR volunteers got finished telling their stories, everyone in town would know what had happened. "Someone deliberately ran them off the road," he said.

Wade's eyes narrowed. "You're kidding me."

"I'm not. Do you know anybody who drives a black truck with a brush guard who might want to do something like that?"

"Half of our customers probably drive black trucks, and a lot of them have brush guards," he said. "Why would someone do something like that?"

"I don't know. But I'm going to find out."

The two men stopped at the elevators. "I'm glad I ran into you," Travis said. "I was going to stop by the store today or tomorrow to talk to you."

"What about?"

"The day Andy was killed—you said you saw a woman going into his office, about the time he would have died."

Wade nodded. "I thought it was Lacy—but I didn't really get a good look at her. I just saw her from the back. She had hair the color of Lacy's and she was the same height and build."

"Is there anything at all about her that you remember—anything that stood out?"

Wade shook his head. "That was more than three years ago," he said. "I couldn't tell you what I had for breakfast last week, so details about something that happened that long ago—they're just not there."

"I know it's a long shot, but if you think of anything, let me know."

"Sure thing. And I hope you find whoever did this to Brenda and Lacy." The elevator doors opened and they stepped in. "I guess the car is pretty wrecked, huh?" Wade asked.

"I imagine the insurance company will total it," Travis said.

"Brock said he saw Bud O'Brien's wrecker hauling it through town. He said looking at it you wouldn't guess anybody could walk away from the crash."

Lacy and Brenda hadn't exactly walked away, but Travis knew what he meant. "They were lucky," he said. "Whoever did this to them won't be when I find him."

"Bud can add the car to the collection at his yard," Wade said.

"We'll go over it for evidence first," Travis said. "I'm hoping the forensics team can get some paint samples from the vehicle that hit them."

"Yeah. I guess they can do all kinds of things like that these days." The door opened on the ground floor. "Good seeing you again, Sheriff."

Travis checked in with the office on his way to his SUV. "Gage put Eddie Carstairs on traffic patrol out on Fireline Road," Adelaide reported. "We had so many rubberneckers driving out there to see the crash site that he was afraid there would be another accident. And Eddie needs the training hours, anyway."

"Good idea," Travis said. "I'm leaving the hospital now. And before you ask, Lacy is banged up but awake and should be going home in the morning. Brenda is in ICU with a head injury and broken ribs, but she should recover fine."

"That poor woman." Adelaide clucked her tongue. "As if she hasn't been through enough already."

"I'm headed back out to the crash site," Travis said. "I know Gage and the crime scene techs already took pictures and measurements, but I want another look on my own. Call if anything urgent comes up."

"Will do, Sheriff."

As he was leaving the parking lot, Travis recognized Wade's truck in front of him. It was red, with the Eagle Mountain Outfitters logo on the tailgate. But Wade wasn't alone. A man sat in the passenger seat. As Wade turned right, Travis got a look at the passenger's profile and recognized Ian. Odd that Wade hadn't mentioned that Ian was with him. Then again, maybe they had been headed somewhere else when Wade decided to swing by the hospital. Wade had said that Ian was uncomfortable around new people, so maybe it wasn't surprising he had decided to wait in the truck.

Travis was halfway back to Eagle Mountain when his phone showed a call from Gage. "We may have found the truck," Gage said when Travis answered. "Though I don't know what good it's going to do us."

Chapter Six

"What do you mean, you don't know how much good the truck will do us?" Travis asked.

"Somebody set it on fire," Gage said. "A hiker saw the smoke and called it in. By the time the volunteer firefighters got there, it was toast. No license plates, and I'm betting when we examine the wreckage we'll find the VIN had been tampered with or removed."

"Where is it?" Travis asked.

Gage gave a location on the edge of a state wilderness area—but still in the sheriff department's jurisdiction. "I'll be there in about forty-five minutes," Travis said.

"I'm going off shift in fifteen minutes," Gage said. "Dwight is coming on to relieve me, but I can stick around if you need me to."

"Don't you have a class tonight?" Travis asked. His brother was studying for the sergeant's exam.

"I do, but I could miss it one time."

"No. Go to your class. Dwight can handle things."

Travis checked the clock on his dash—almost three, and he hadn't eaten since breakfast. He swung through a drive-through for a chicken burrito to go, then headed out to view this burned-out truck.

A fire truck and crew stood watching the smoldering remains of the blaze when Travis pulled up, along with Sheriff's Deputy Dwight Prentice. Dwight walked out to meet the sheriff. A rangy young officer who walked with the shambling, slightly bowlegged gait of a man who had spent most of his life on horseback, Dwight had surprised everyone when he had decided to seek a career in law enforcement after his return from active duty in Afghanistan, rather than take over the family ranch. "Good afternoon, Sheriff," he said when Travis climbed out of his SUV.

Travis nodded and looked toward the blackened remains of what had once been a pickup truck, the metal frame and parts of the seats and engine still visible amid the ashes. "That was about all that was left of it when I arrived," Dwight said.

The two men walked closer. Tendrils of smoke curled up from the wreckage and heat still radiated from it. "And why do we think this is the truck we've been looking for?" Travis asked.

"The hikers who called in the fire said it was a late-model black Chevy," Dwight said. "With a brush guard. You can still see the guard up front there."

The brush guard lay in the ashes near the front of the truck, blackened but intact. "Something like that would make it easy to ram another vehicle without tearing up your own ride," Dwight said.

"But we still don't know that this is the truck," Travis said.

"True," Dwight said. "But it looks like the fire was deliberate."

"Oh, it was deliberate, all right." Assistant Fire Chief Tom Reynolds joined them. "You can see they loaded up the bed with gas cans before they lit it." He pointed to the twisted remains of the cans in front of the rear axle. "The hikers said they heard a big explosion, and a couple of other people called it in, too."

"Adelaide said one woman called the station and wanted to know if they were blasting up at the Lazy Susan Mine again," Dwight said. "And it's been shut down for thirty years."

"I reckon whoever did this stood way back and set the fire by firing a flare gun into the gas cans," Tom said. "As soon as everything cools down enough to search, we'll get our arson investigator in here. He might be able to find the remains of the flare."

Travis nodded and looked around them. The country up here was pretty desolate—rocky and covered with knots of Gambel oak scrub, prickly pear cactus and stunted juniper trees. In the fall, hunters swarmed the area hoping to bag a mule deer or elk, but this time of year the only people who came to the area were more adventurous hikers, looking for a challenging route over Dakota Ridge, which rose on the horizon to the north. "If somebody drove the truck up here to dump it, then set it on fire, how did they leave? Did the hikers report seeing another vehicle?"

"Gage asked them that and they said no," Dwight said. "But it's possible they weren't in a position to see the road, so whoever did this could have had a second vehicle waiting to drive away. Or they could have walked out cross-county." He gestured past the burned-out vehicle. "There are a couple of trails you can access from here that will take you back to the highway. It would only be a hike of three or four miles."

"We'll ask around, but I'm not holding out a lot of hope." He turned to Tom. "When is the arson investigator coming out?"

"Tomorrow morning. It would be a good idea if you posted someone here to guard the scene until we can give it a good look."

"I'll stay here until my shift ends at midnight," Dwight said. "Then Eddie will relieve me."

"I thought Eddie was on traffic duty on Fireline Road," Travis said.

"Gage sent him home, since the lookie-loos had apparently had enough. He told him to come back out here at midnight to relieve me."

"All right." Travis studied the still-smoldering wreckage. "What do you think a late-model Chevy is worth these days?"

"Depends on how old, but thirty or forty thousand at least."

"That's a lot of money to burn up," Travis said. "If this is the truck we were looking for, somebody was willing to get rid of it rather than risk getting caught."

"Some people will do anything to avoid going to jail," Dwight said.

"A good lawyer would try to plead down to reckless driving. Someone without a record might get off with probation and community service, maybe lose their license for a while."

"Or somebody who already had a criminal record might be looking at serious time," Dwight said.

"Or whoever did this is involved in something else they don't want us to find out about." Travis shook his head.

"Do you think this is connected to Andy Stenson's murder?" Dwight asked.

"Do you?" Travis asked.

Dwight nudged his Stetson farther back on his head. "Brenda is Andy's widow. Lacy was the woman everyone thought killed him. Targeting them seems like more than a coincidence. Maybe the real killer thinks they know something—or could learn something—that would point back to him or her."

"Maybe," Travis said. "Which makes me think the sooner I can see what's in Andy's files, the better."

"Every inch of me hurts, but I don't even care, I'm just so glad to be alive." Lacy sat on the wicker settee on her parents' front porch, a bowl of popcorn on one side of her, a glass of lemonade on the other, talking to her attorney, Anisha Cook, on the phone. The sweet scent of peonies drifted to her on the breeze and in spite of everything, she felt happier than she had since she had walked out of the door of the Denver Women's Correctional Facility. Although, who was to say some of that wasn't due to the painkillers the hospital had sent her home with?

"Do the police know who did this?" Anisha asked. "Are the drivers that bad over on your side of the Divide?"

Some of Lacy's euphoria evaporated. "Whoever did this deliberately hit us," she said. "I don't think the chances are very good that the police will find them, though Travis is apparently out questioning anyone and everyone."

"Travis? Do you mean Sheriff Travis Walker?"

"Yes. He seems to be taking this attack on me personally."

"Well, that is in-ter-est-ing." Anisha drew out the last word, a hint of laughter in her voice. "Looks like he's appointed himself your personal knight in shining armor."

"Don't be ridiculous." The settee creaked as Lacy shifted position.

"It's no secret he feels guilty about what happened to you," Anisha said. "I had my doubts when he first came to me with the evidence he had found to clear you, but I think he might be the genuine article."

"What do you mean?" Lacy asked.

"A nice guy. And he's definitely easy on the eyes."

Lacy's cheeks felt hot, and she was glad Anisha wasn't here to see her. "You didn't call me to talk about Travis Walker," she said.

"No. I have some good news for you."

"What is it?"

"The state is cutting you a check for $210,000."

Lacy almost dropped the phone. "What?"

"It's the money they owe you for your wrongful incarceration—seventy thousand dollars a year for three years. All duly authorized by state law."

Lacy collapsed against the back of the settee. "I don't know what to say," she said. "I'm stunned."

"It's no less than you deserve," Anisha said. "It's money for you to use to start over. Maybe you want to use it for your education, to start a new career."

"I don't know what I want to do," Lacy said. "I haven't had time to think."

"There's always law," Anisha said. "I can recommend some good schools."

Lacy laughed. "I'm so grateful for everything you've done for me, but I'm not sure I'm cut out to be a lawyer. I'll have to think."

"You do that. And let me know if the check doesn't show up in a couple of days. They're supposed to be sending it directly to you."

Lacy ended the call and sat back, trying to

let the news sink in. The money didn't feel real yet, but then, nothing about her situation did.

The door into the house opened and her mother stepped out onto the porch. "How are you doing out here?" she asked. "Do you need anything?"

"I'm doing well," Lacy said. "Great, even. I just heard from Anisha. The state is paying me a bunch of money. I guess there's a state law that says they have to."

Jeanette hugged her daughter. "That's wonderful. I'm so happy for you." She sat next to Lacy.

"I should use the money to pay you and Dad back for all you've done for me," Lacy said. "I know you took out a second mortgage on this house to pay my legal bills, and you used your savings…"

"Don't say another word." Jeanette put a hand over Lacy's. "We want you to use the money for your education, and for things you need—a car, maybe, or a place to live, though you are welcome to stay here as long as you like."

Lacy nodded. She would need all those things, wouldn't she? After so many months with no hope, she was going to have to get used to planning for the future again.

A familiar black-and-white SUV moved slowly down the street toward them. Lacy's heart sped up, though not, she had to admit, from fear. She no longer feared Travis Walker. And she had stopped hating him. But she wasn't indifferent to him, either. She couldn't decide where he fit in her categorization of people. He wasn't her enemy anymore, but was she ready to accept him as a friend?

Travis parked at the curb and strode up the walkway, confident and oh-so-masculine. He was one of those men who never looked rumpled or out of shape. "Good afternoon, ladies." He touched the brim of his Stetson. "I heard they let you out of the hospital, Lacy. How are you feeling?"

"Sore, but I'll live. Too bad it isn't Halloween, though. My face could be my costume."

He leaned closer to examine her face. "The bruises are turning Technicolor," he said. "Better start embellishing your story. Who did you say beat you in that boxing match?"

Lacy laughed in spite of herself. So much for keeping her emotions in check around this man. "What brings you here?" she asked. "Or did you just stop by to see how I'm doing?"

"I thought I should let you know the latest on the case, before the news got back to you through the Eagle Mountain grapevine."

"Eagle Mountain has a grapevine?" she asked.

"You know it. And half the time it starts in my office, with Adelaide Kinkaid."

"Sit down, Travis." Jeanette pulled up a chair. "Tell us what you've found out."

He sat. "We think we found the truck that ran you off the road," he said. "Someone drove it to an isolated area and set it on fire. We can't be 100 percent sure that it's the right one, but we think so. The Vehicle Identification Number was removed and there were no license plates. I don't know if we'll ever identify the owner."

"I wish you could find him," Jeanette said. "I hate thinking someone like that is out there, running free."

"We're doing the best we can," Travis said.

"I know that. And we appreciate it." She stood. "I have to get back to work. You stay and talk to Lacy."

They waited until her mother had shut the door behind her before either of them said anything. "I talked to—" she began.

"How are you—" he said.

"You first," he said, and motioned for her to continue.

"I talked to Brenda today," Lacy said. "She was pretty groggy, but awake. She thinks the doctors will let her go home tomorrow or the next day."

"That's great news."

"I got some more good news," she said. "The state is paying me a settlement. Apparently they have to, according to state law."

"I guess I had heard something about that," he said. "I'm glad. You can use the money to make a fresh start."

"I'm still trying to decide what to do with the money, but it does feel good to know it's there."

"I spoke to a friend of yours this morning," he said, a teasing glint in his eye.

"Oh? Who was that?"

"Alvin Exeter. We had an appointment, remember?"

"And what did he have to say?"

"I told him I knew he wasn't writing a piece on rural law enforcement and that I wouldn't talk to him about anything else. He said I must have spoken to you, but that refusing to do an interview with him wouldn't stop the book. He told me if I cooperated and spoke to him, he would be sure to present my side of the story. Otherwise I could come off looking like a stupid hick cop who took the easy way out on a case and got it wrong."

"He threatened you!" she said. "What a miserable worm. If I see him again—"

Travis's hand on her arm silenced her. "He isn't that wrong, you know," he said. "I did take the easy way out and I did get it wrong."

"You were inexperienced." She said the words without thinking. But she realized they were true. She had been twenty when she was sentenced for murder, but Travis had only been twenty-three. And he had never handled a murder case before.

"I should have done a better job," he said. "I will this time."

Lacy believed him, and she vowed to do what she could to help him. After all, she would only be helping herself. "I've been thinking about what happened," she said. "I have to wonder if whoever ran us off the road did so because he didn't want us to examine those files. It wouldn't be that difficult to figure out what we were doing out at Andy's storage unit. If he was watching us, he would have seen us put the files in Brenda's car."

Travis nodded. "I've thought of that, too."

"Where are the files now?" she asked.

"They're in my SUV." He nodded toward the vehicle parked at the curb. "I'm not trying to rush you, but when you're ready, I'd like to go through them."

"I'm ready now." She stood, fighting not to show how much it hurt.

"You just came home from the hospital," he protested.

"And I'm going nuts, sitting here doing nothing. Trust me, this is just what I need to distract me."

Chapter Seven

Lacy waited on the porch while Travis retrieved both boxes from the car and she held the door while he carried them inside. "Go through that archway on the right," she said. "We can use the dining table."

She flicked the light switch as she followed him into the room, illuminating the chandelier that cast a golden glow over the cherry dining set for eight that the family only used for holidays and formal occasions. Travis set the boxes on the table. "I'll be right back," he said, and went out again.

He returned moments later, carrying a video camera on a tripod. "This is probably overkill," he said as he positioned the camera. "But I didn't want to take any chances."

Camera in place and running, he broke the seal on the first box and removed the lid. The first file he opened on the table between them was the contract Henry Hake had signed, as president and CEO of Hake Development, with Andrew Stenson as his legal representative in the matter of Eagle Mountain Resort, a high-altitude luxury resort development.

"I remember the day Andy signed that contract," Lacy said. "He took me and Brenda to lunch and insisted on ordering champagne. We teased him that he was going to get a reputation as a lush, drinking at noon."

"It was a big contract for a fairly new lawyer," Travis said.

"The biggest. And totally out of the blue. We couldn't believe our luck when Mr. Hake contacted us. He said he wanted someone fresh, with new ideas, and that he believed in supporting local talent."

"Still, this development looks like a big deal," Travis said. "I'm surprised he didn't want someone who was more experienced in real estate law." He removed a folded paper from an envelope labeled Plat and spread it across the table. "Tell me about this," he said.

Lacy leaned over his shoulder, the soap and starch scent of him sending a tingle through her midsection. She forced herself to focus on the plat of the development, instead of on the way his shoulders stretched tight the crisp cotton of his uniform shirt, or the way his dark hair curled up at the collar, exposing a scant half inch of skin…

"These were all old mining claims, right?" Travis prompted.

"Right. Mining claims." She swallowed and shifted her gaze to the blue lines on the creamy paper. "Hake Development was able to buy up approximately fifty mining claims, all above nine thousand feet, an area that has traditionally been deemed unsuitable for development."

"Why is that?" Travis asked.

"Mostly because there's so much snow up there in the winter it makes it difficult to maintain roads," Lacy said. "Plus, there's a higher avalanche danger. Up at the higher elevations, above treeline, the ground is tundra, frozen year-round. That makes it unstable to build on. Hake had engineers who had devised plans for getting around those limitations—foundations anchored on rock deep in the ground, regular avalanche mitigation, roads on traditional mining trails, water piped up from far below in an elaborate network of aqueducts."

Travis whistled. "Sounds expensive."

"Oh, it was. But Hake swore he knew plenty of people who would pay a premium price to live with the kind of views and privacy you get at those elevations."

"Not everyone was thrilled about his plans, I'm sure."

"Oh, no. The Ute Indian tribe objected because some of that terrain overlaps areas they deem sacred. And the environmentalists were in an uproar over the potential damage to fragile tundra. They succeeded in getting an injunction to stop the development until environmental studies could be done."

"And were the studies done?" he asked.

"I don't know," she said. "But we could probably find out." The idea excited her. She had missed this—working on something constructive, researching and finding out things, instead of simply sitting back and letting each day stretch forward with no goal or purpose.

"You find out what you can about the injunction and any studies," Travis said. "Meanwhile, I'll talk to Henry Hake, and ask him to update us on the project."

"My mom said they haven't built anything up here," Lacy said. "Maybe he couldn't beat the injunction. Or he decided the project was too expensive to pursue. He supposedly had a lot of investors who wanted to put money into the resort, but maybe the injunction caused them to change their minds."

"I'll find out." He pulled another stack of

files from the box and handed her half. "Let's see if anything stands out in these."

As Lacy read through the contents, it was as if she was sitting back in the little office on Fourth Street, twenty years old and ready to take on the world, excited to have found interesting work right here in Eagle Mountain, the place she loved best in the world. From the window by her desk she could look up and see Dakota Ridge, and the road leading out of town, Mount Rayford peeking up over the ridge, snowcapped year-round.

As she flipped through the files, she remembered typing memos and motions, and discussing the work with Andy over sandwiches at their desks. Sometimes Brenda would stop by to say hello and share a story about her work at the history museum. Though the world hadn't been perfect back then, it had sure seemed so at times.

"Find anything interesting?" Travis asked after they had been reading silently for almost an hour.

"Not really," she said. "Most of it is just routine stuff—surveyor's reports and court motions, tax paperwork—nothing out of the ordinary. How about you?"

"I found this." He pushed a piece of paper across to her. "Any idea what it means?"

The note was written on the blank side of a "While You Were Out" message slip. *Ask Hake about notes.*

Lacy made a face. "This is Andy's handwriting, but I don't know what notes he's referring to."

Travis set the paper aside and they searched through the rest of the first box. Lacy could tell when her pain medication wore off, as her head began to throb, her vision blurring from the pain. She put a hand to her temple, grimacing. "We should stop now," Travis said. "We can do the other box later."

"I guess you're right." Fatigue dragged at her—she could have put her head down and gone to sleep right there beside him.

"I appreciate your help," Travis said. "But don't overdo it."

She nodded. "What will you do now?" she asked.

Travis picked up the slip of paper he had set aside earlier. "I think I'll start by asking Hake about this."

GETTING AN INTERVIEW with Henry Hake proved to be more difficult than Travis had expected. When he had telephoned the number for Hake Development yesterday, a brisk-sounding woman informed him that Mr. Hake was out of town. "I can ask him to call you when he returns," she said. "But it may be some time before you hear from him."

"This is a police matter. I need to hear from him sooner, rather than later."

"Oh. Well, I'll certainly let him know."

"So you're sure you don't know when he'll be back in town."

The silence on the other end of the line went on so long Travis wondered if they had lost their connection. "Are you still there?" he asked.

"Mr. Hake may be back tomorrow—but you didn't hear that from me."

"What's the status of the Eagle Mountain Resort development?" Travis asked.

"I don't have any information on that to give you," she said.

"Is that because you don't know or because the official policy is to keep silent?" he asked.

"I'm sure I don't know what you mean," she said. "Is there anything else I can help you with?"

"No, thank you." He ended the call, then called Adelaide. "I need you to track down Henry Hake's personal number and address."

"Will do, Sheriff."

Travis turned to his computer and found a report from the county's arson investigator in his inbox. He settled back to read, finding no surprises. The truck was a standard model, probably from the last two or three years, judging by what little remained of the frame and engine. No VIN, no plates. The only nonstandard feature was the brush guard, which had been welded of heavy pipe and wasn't the sort of thing that could be ordered from a catalog. Travis called Adelaide again. "Who's on shift right now?" he asked.

"Dwight just came on. He's probably still in the parking lot, if you need him for something."

"See if you can grab him and tell him I want to talk to him for a minute."

A few minutes later, Dwight entered Travis's office. "What can I do for you, Sheriff?"

"I need you to check with any metal fabricators or welders around here, see if any of them made a brush guard like this for a guy with a black Chevy pickup." He slid a note across the desk with the description and dimensions of the brush guard.

"Sure." Dwight pocketed the note. "This have anything to do with the guy that ran Lacy Milligan and Brenda Stenson off Fireline Road?" he asked.

"Yes. I'm hoping we'll get lucky and turn up a lead, but it's a long shot."

Dwight hesitated in the doorway. "Is there something else?" Travis asked.

"I was just wondering how Mrs. Stenson is doing?" Dwight said. "I heard she was hurt pretty bad in the accident."

"She's doing much better," Travis said. "She should get to come home in a few days."

Dwight nodded, his expression solemn. "I'm glad to hear it. She and I were in school together. She was always a real sweet girl."

Dwight left and Travis sat back in his chair, staring at the computer, wondering what he should do next. He was tempted to call Lacy and brainstorm with her about the case—or better yet, go by and see her. He discarded the idea immediately. Though she had seemed to enjoy the time they had spent together, he wasn't going to delude himself into thinking she was helping him out of anything other than self-interest. Maybe once upon a time the two of them could have hit it off and been a couple. But too much had come between them now.

"Why are you sitting there with that moony look on your face?"

Travis looked up to find his brother standing in the doorway of his office. He sat up straight and assumed his best all-business expression. "I just sent Dwight out to try to track down the welder who made the brush guard on that burned-out truck," he said. "And I've got a call in to Henry Hake, trying to find out about a note we found in Andy Stenson's files."

"I thought Hake was out of town," Gage said.

"When I pressed his assistant, she admitted that he's supposed to return today."

"So you've been busy." Gage crossed to the visitor's chair across from the desk and sat. "When this is all over—when we've closed the case—are you going to ask her out?"

"Ask who out?" Travis stared at his computer screen, the words of the arson investigator's report blurring together.

"Lacy. And don't lie to me and say you aren't gone over her. You acted this same way about Didi Samuelson. I recognize the signs."

"Didi Samuelson was in eighth grade," Travis protested.

"Which only proves that love reduces all of us to immature shadows of ourselves," Gage said.

"And you know this because you've been in love so much."

Gage stretched his arms over his head. "I know this because I've studied how to successfully avoid falling victim to the dreaded love disease," he said. "And stop trying to change the subject. We're talking about you here, not me."

"I am not in love with Lacy Milligan." Travis kept his voice down, hoping Adelaide wasn't listening in, but doubting he would be so lucky. The woman had ears like a cat's. "I hardly know her."

"Right. So you only tied yourself in knots and practically killed yourself clearing her name because you wanted to do the right thing."

"Yes. Of course. I would have done that for anyone."

Gage laughed. "Pardon me if I have a hard time believing you would have gotten quite so worked up about some ugly guy with tattoos and a rap sheet as long as my arm."

"I made a mistake arresting her and I had to make up for it."

Gage leaned forward, his expression no longer mocking. "You did your job," he said. "You arrested her because the evidence pointed to her as the perpetrator of the crime."

"It was a sloppy investigation. The follow-up proved that. The money missing from the business account was a bookkeeping error. The money in Lacy's account really was from selling her grandmother's ring. She really wasn't in town at the time Andy was killed. If I had done my job and taken a closer look at the evidence, I would have found that out."

"You know what they say—hindsight is

twenty-twenty. You could have looked at that evidence ten times back then and you might not have seen anything different."

"But I might have," Travis said. That knowledge would haunt him for the rest of his life. It had changed the way he looked at every case now.

"I know one thing," Gage said. "This whole situation has made you a better cop. And it's made all of us who work under you better cops."

"Yeah, it taught you not to make the mistakes I did," Travis said.

Gage sat back again. "And it taught us to man up and admit it when we do make a mistake, and to do what we can to right the wrong."

"Glad I could be such a shining example," Travis said sourly.

Gage stood and hitched up his utility belt. "Lacy is still speaking to you, in spite of everything," he said. "That has to be a good sign."

"She's a good person."

"And so are you. Don't sell yourself short. I'm not saying you have to rush things, but don't give up before you start." He pointed a finger at Travis. "You taught me that, too."

He left the office. Travis stared after him, an unsettled feeling in his chest he wasn't sure he wanted to examine too closely. It could be his brother had stirred up something inside him—something like hope.

BRENDA CAME HOME from the hospital the next day, and the day after that Lacy delivered a box of fancy chocolates and a chicken casserole to her friend's door. "The casserole is from my mom, but the chocolates are from me," Lacy said as she carried her gifts into Brenda's house. It was the same house she and Andy had purchased shortly after moving to Eagle Mountain—a former forest ranger's residence originally built by the Civilian Conservation Corps in the 1930s, constructed of native stone and cedar, with hand-carved shutters and door lintels. They had updated the house with new windows and roof and a new heating system, part of the improvements paid for with money from Henry Hake's retainer.

"Thank you for both," Brenda said, gingerly lowering herself to the sofa.

"It still hurts, doesn't it?" Lacy asked, as Brenda sucked in her breath and winced.

"The doctor taped the ribs, but all I can do is wait for them to heal," Brenda said. "I still get dizzy from the head injury, and I can't read for long without getting a headache. The neurologist said those symptoms could take months to disappear, though she reassured me there's no permanent damage."

"That's going to make it tough at work, isn't it?" Lacy asked.

"Jan already called and told me not to worry. I know not everyone gets along with her, but ever since Andy died, she's been an absolute peach." She leaned forward to study Lacy's face. "You look pretty beat up yourself," she said. "How are you feeling?"

"Much better, actually," Lacy said. "The headaches are almost gone. I'm still a little stiff and sore, but that will go away eventually." She made a face. "I was hoping makeup would cover the worst of the bruising, but no such luck."

"You're still beautiful and it makes you look… I don't know—tough."

"That would have come in handy when I was in prison." At Brenda's stricken look, Lacy laughed. "It's okay, really," she said. "I don't mind talking about it. I figure better to get it out in the open and own it than to worry everyone's talking about it behind my back—which you know they are."

"I guess people are curious," Brenda said weakly.

"Of course they are. I would be, too. So

don't be afraid to ask me questions. I'll answer if I can."

Brenda shook her head. "I don't want to know anything. All I care about is that you're here now. Though if I could ask a question of someone, I would want to know who tried to kill us the other day. And why?"

"Travis is following every lead, but he hasn't come up with much yet," Lacy said. "He and I started going through some of Andy's files, hoping we could find some clue—in case the guy who hit us was trying to stop us from looking through the files."

"Did you find anything?" Brenda asked.

"Only a note on the back of a 'While You Were Out' slip. It was in Andy's handwriting, and it said, 'Ask Hake about the notes.' Do you have any idea what that might mean?"

Brenda frowned. "I have no idea what it means. You know Andy—he was always making notes to himself about things he wanted to do or find out. For weeks after he died I would find little scraps of paper around the house."

"I'm sorry," Lacy said. "I didn't mean to upset you."

"No, it's okay." She straightened her shoulders. "It's actually been a lot better since you came home. I think I had that burden of guilt hanging over me, keeping me from moving on."

"I'd think it would be easier to move on if you knew who actually killed Andy," Lacy said.

"It would. But I'm getting used to the idea that that might never happen. I still have to live my life, so that's what I'm trying to do."

"You're still young. Maybe one day you'll meet another man you can love."

"Maybe. Though dating in a small town can be problematic."

"You mean, you can't really keep a relationship secret," Lacy said. "But at least we're luckier than some places. Single men still outnumber single women in these mountain towns, so we have a better selection to choose from."

"I don't care about a selection," Brenda said. "I just want to find the one right guy. But enough about me. How many guys have asked you out since you came home?"

Lacy blinked. "None. Why would they?"

"Hello? Didn't we just say there are more single men than women around here? And here you are, a beautiful young woman who hasn't had a date in at least three years. I'm surprised they aren't lined up at your door."

Once again, Lacy cursed her tendency to blush so easily. "I was single before I went to prison, too," she said. "And I never dated that much." In fact, she had never had a serious relationship. She had always put it down to men seeing her more as a best friend than as a lover.

"There's a new guy in town who looks pretty interesting," Brenda said. "I saw him with Brock Ryan at the climbing wall in Ute Park when I cut through there to deliver an ad to the *Examiner* office. He was about halfway up the wall and, well, I'm not ashamed to admit I stopped and stared. And I wasn't the only one. The two of them had drawn quite an audience of female admirers. Adelaide Kinkaid was there, too."

"Adelaide is old enough to be Brock's grandmother," Lacy said.

"You'd have to be dead not to notice those two," Brenda said. "I mean, Brock is good-looking, but this new guy…" She fanned herself. "He was like a statue of some Greek god. Amazing."

"Then I hope I get a chance to check him out," Lacy said. "What's his name?"

"Tammy Patterson at the paper told me his name is Ian Barnes. He's a veteran and she thinks he's in town visiting Brock and staying at his place. She tried to get him to do an interview with her for the paper, but he wasn't interested."

"I don't guess I know Tammy," Lacy said.

"She moved here last year from Minnesota.

Sweet kid, fresh out of college. She works weekends at Moe's Pub."

"That sounds like a good place to run into good-looking men," Lacy said.

"Except Tammy is apparently engaged to her high school sweetheart back in Duluth and staying true to him," Brenda said. "Which doesn't keep the men in town from pursuing her. I guess playing hard to get really is an effective strategy."

"You really do know all the gossip," Lacy said. "Is that because you've been studying, preparing to dive back into the dating game?"

"It's really because Jan keeps tabs on everything and everyone in town, and passes the information on to me," Brenda said. "She may not be mayor of Eagle Mountain anymore, but she still wants to know what's going on."

"I was surprised to find out she didn't run for reelection when her term ended," Lacy said. "She seemed to enjoy the job so much, and she was good at it."

"She said it was time to move on to something else. And Larry had already declared his intention to run, and he seemed really serious about wanting the job, so I guess she figured it was a good time to bow out."

"Maybe we should talk to her about Andy," Lacy said. "Maybe she knows something about the mysterious woman Brock saw near his office the day he died, or someone with a black truck who might have had it in for us."

"She holds court at a back table at Kate's Kitchen every Thursday morning," Brenda said. "We could go there tomorrow if you like."

"I would like, if you're up to it."

"It's a date, then." Brenda picked up the box of chocolates. "Now, let's try out your gift. I get dibs on the caramels."

Chapter Eight

Henry Hake lived in a stone-and-cedar mansion near the base of Mount Rayford. A black iron gate blocked the winding paved drive, so Travis parked and called Hake's private number on his cell phone. "Hello?" The voice that answered was hesitant and higher-pitched than Travis had expected.

"This is Rayford County Sheriff Travis Walker. I need you to open the gate so I can come up and see you."

"What is this about?"

"We'll discuss that when I get there. Open the gate, please."

"I really don't have time for this. I'm on my way out."

"Then you shouldn't waste any more time discussing this. Open the gate and I'll be out of your way as quickly as possible." Silence stretched between them, but Travis could hear the other man breathing and knew he hadn't disconnected. He resisted the temptation to speak, letting the tension build. Finally, the gate groaned and began to swing open.

"I'll be up in a minute," Travis said, and ended the call.

He returned to his car and drove the quarter mile up to the house. Hake met him at the door. "Hurry. I don't have time to waste," he said, ushering Travis inside. A portly man in a light gray suit with worn cuffs, Henry Hake looked more like a schoolteacher than a millionaire businessman. Travis followed him down a mahogany-paneled hallway to a small, dark office, where Hake took a seat behind a cluttered desk. Dust coated the side tables and floated in the shaft of sunlight from the single window, where a leggy geranium sprawled across the sill. "What do you want?" Hake asked.

"I want to talk to you about Andy Stenson," he said.

Hake blinked. He clearly hadn't been expecting this topic of conversation. "What about him? He's dead."

"I'm trying to find out who killed him."

"Got that wrong the first time, didn't you?" Hake pawed through the papers on the desk until he unearthed a cell phone. He stared at the screen, then back up at Travis. "You've got five minutes."

"Why did you hire Andy Stenson to represent you and Eagle Mountain Resort?" Travis asked. "Why not a more experienced lawyer?"

"I wanted to give the kid a chance."

"Did you know him previously? How did you decide on him?"

"Never heard of the kid. A business associate suggested it."

"Who is this business associate?"

"That doesn't really matter. You're wasting your time."

The five-minute deadline was a bluff, Travis decided. As far as he could tell, Hake was alone in the house. It wasn't likely he could throw Travis out by himself. "What's the status of Eagle Mountain Resort?" he asked.

"We're restructuring."

"Who is we?"

"I have business partners—some of whom prefer to remain silent."

"You went to a lot of trouble to buy up the mining claims and develop plans for the resort. Why didn't you go through with them?"

"I really can't talk about that."

"Why not?"

Hake snatched the phone from his desk and shoved it into the inside pocket of his jacket. "It ought to be obvious to you, if you've done any investigating, that someone doesn't want that project to go forward."

"Who?" Travis asked. "The environmentalists?"

"Maybe. There was some sabotage that might have been their doing. What do they call it—monkey-wrenching? We had equipment destroyed, some property stolen."

Travis hadn't heard any of this. "Did you report this to the police?"

"We didn't want the bad publicity. We handled it ourselves by posting private security. After that we didn't have any more troubles."

"Who is we?"

Hake waved a hand as if shooing a fly. "The organization. Who doesn't really matter."

Travis took Andy's note from his pocket and passed it to Hake. "What can you tell me about this?"

Hake studied it. "What is this? It doesn't make sense."

"I found it in Andy Stenson's files."

Hake tossed the paper back toward Travis. "I have no idea what it's about."

Travis had given a lot of thought to what the note might mean. He risked a guess. "Was someone writing you threatening letters? Is that what Andy wanted to know more about?"

Hake's face registered an internal struggle.

"There were a couple of nasty notes," he said finally. "I never should have mentioned them to Andy, but I thought it would be a good idea if someone knew—for insurance."

"Do you think Andy decided to look into the threats on his own?" Travis said. "Is that what led to his death?"

Hake pushed out his lower lip. He had a cut on his chin, maybe from shaving. "I wondered at first, if maybe he had gotten too close to someone who didn't want to be found out."

"Why didn't you say something?" Travis tried to rein in his anger. "Your suspicions might have led us to look at other suspects in the murder."

"I thought if I opened my mouth whoever had killed Andy would come after me next."

"Who do you think killed him?" Travis leaned toward him. "If you have any ideas, tell me."

"I don't know who. And if I did, I'm smart enough to keep my mouth shut. I was so terrified at the time, I hired a bodyguard."

"Who did you hire?" Maybe the bodyguard knew more about these threats.

"A professional. He came highly recommended, but I don't remember his name. He didn't work for me for long."

"Why not?"

"After Andy died, the threats went away. The injunction stopped the development, so I guess our opponents got what they wanted."

"I'll need the names of your business partners so that I can talk to them, too. Maybe they know more about the source of the threats."

"They don't know anything, I promise. Some of them aren't even alive anymore, and the others won't talk to you."

"Tell me their names, anyway."

"I'm sorry, I really can't help you. And I have another appointment." He rose.

Travis stood, also. "Did you keep any of the threatening notes you received?" he asked.

"No. I destroyed them a long time ago."

"And you have no idea who sent them?"

"None. As I said, it happened a long time ago." His eyes met Travis's. "I've put it behind me, and you should, too."

He walked Travis to the front door. As Travis drove away from the mansion, Hake's final words replayed in his head. Was the developer merely offering advice, or was he making a threat?

Lacy and Brenda walked into Kate's Kitchen a few minutes after nine o'clock the next morning and found Jan Selkirk having coffee with Adelaide Kinkaid and two other women at a table near the back. The former mayor—a striking, fortysomething woman with big brown eyes and ash-blond hair in a tumble of curls around her shoulders—looked up and smiled at their approach. "Good morning, Brenda. I didn't expect to see you out and about so soon."

"I was going crazy, sitting around the house," Brenda said. She pulled out a chair and carefully lowered herself into it. "You know Lacy Milligan, don't you?"

Lacy leaned forward and offered her hand.

"I do. It's been a while," Jan said, with a firm handshake. "I hope you won't be offended, dear, but you look like you took a real beating. I'm so sorry. And the police have no idea who attacked you two?"

"If there's a clue to be found, Travis will find it," Adelaide said. "The poor man is working himself into the ground." She studied Lacy over her coffee cup. "I thought things would settle down once he got Lacy home, but I guess we're not going to be so lucky."

Lacy tried not to resent the implication that she was personally responsible for a new local crime wave. She took the chair next to Brenda and accepted the carafe of coffee one of the women passed her.

"We have a few questions since, as former

mayor, you know pretty much everyone in town," Brenda said.

"What you mean is that she has the dirt on everyone," Adelaide said. She pushed out her chair and stood. "Come on, ladies. Let's leave these young women to it. I need to get to the station, anyway. If I don't, Gage will make the coffee and it will be so strong you could strip paint with it."

When Lacy and Brenda were alone with Jan, the older woman leaned back in her chair and studied them. "What do you want to know?" she asked.

"At my trial, Wade Tomlinson testified that he saw a woman outside Andy's office about the time Andy was killed—a woman who looked like me," Lacy said. "Obviously, that wasn't me, so do you know who it might have been?"

"I have no idea," Jan said. "I was too busy being mayor at the time to pay attention to anything that didn't pertain to the job."

"Yes, but can you think of anyone who was living in the area at the time—or visiting— who looked like Lacy?" Brenda asked. "A slim young woman with dark hair?"

Jan put a hand to her own blond locks. "No one comes to mind," she said. "It could have been anyone."

"Maybe she was a client of Andy's," Lacy said. "I've tried to think if any of his clients had dark hair, but it was too long ago. I'm hoping when Travis and I look at the rest of Andy's files, it will jog my memory."

"You and Travis are going through Andy's files?" Jan looked amused. "I'll bet that's interesting. As I remember, there was no love lost between you and our young sheriff."

"We've decided to keep the past in the past," Lacy said, eyes downcast. No sense letting the town gossips think anything differently. Lacy's feelings about Travis were so all over the map she didn't need other people weighing in with their opinions.

"What about a newish black truck with a welded brush guard?" Brenda asked. "Do you know anyone with a truck like that?"

"Only half the ranchers in the county," Jan said. "I heard they found the one they think hit you burned out over on the edge of the public land out toward Dakota Ridge."

"Yes, but they don't know who was driving it," Lacy said.

"Whoever it is, let's hope he doesn't try again," Jan said. "Frankly, if I were you two I wouldn't want to be seen out in public together."

"Why do you say that?" Brenda asked.

"Well, since there's no way of putting it delicately, I'll just say it—you don't know who this maniac was really after, do you—you or Lacy. If you're not the one he wants, why take chances hanging out with the one he does?"

Lacy was still trying to digest this take on the situation when the door to the restaurant opened and a man entered. He wore a black watch cap, along with a black T-shirt that fit like a second skin, showing off every chiseled muscle of his shoulders and torso. Every female head in the room—including the two waitresses and the woman at the cash register—swiveled to track his progress to a table by the window. Jan leaned forward. "That's Ian Barnes," she said softly. "Now that is one beautiful man."

"I don't know," Lacy said, turning her back to him. "He's almost too beautiful. And does he ever smile? He looks almost...dangerous."

"Mmmm," Jan purred. "Some women like men like that. And you may not be interested in him, but he's definitely interested in you. He's looking right at you."

Lacy shifted in her chair. "I wish he wouldn't," she said. "Maybe someone should point out that it's rude to stare. He makes me nervous."

"He doesn't drive a black truck," Jan said. "I saw him yesterday in a beat-up Jeep." She sat back and sipped her coffee. "But I swear I've seen him somewhere before. That's not a body—or a face—a woman forgets. But I can't put my finger on where." She shrugged. "I'm sure it will come to me."

The door opened and a second man entered. Lacy let out a groan and turned back around. "Do you know him?" Jan asked.

"His name is Alvin Exeter," Lacy said. "He's a writer who says he's working on a book about me."

"I don't just say it, I'm writing it." Alvin stopped behind Lacy's chair, and the thought passed through her mind that this was what it must feel like for a mouse when a hawk hovered over it. Except she wasn't a mouse.

She turned to look up at the man. "Go away," she said.

"No." He pulled out the chair on her other side and sat.

"I don't have anything to say to you," Lacy said.

"I didn't come to talk to you. I came to talk to Ms. Selkirk."

"Oh?" Jan looked interested. "What about?"

"I understand you were mayor of Eagle Mountain when Andy Stenson was murdered," Alvin said. "I thought you would be the perfect person to give me a picture of what life was like here during that time."

Jan glanced at Lacy, then smiled at Alvin, coral-lipsticked mouth stretched over big teeth. "I'm sorry, Mr. Exeter, but you'll have to write your book without my help. In fact, I think Lacy should write her own book. After all, it's her story to tell."

"Maybe I will," Lacy said, taking her cue, though she had no intention of reliving the last three years on paper.

Alvin's expression turned stormy. "If you don't help me, you have no say in how you're portrayed," he said.

"You're assuming we care," Jan said.

He shoved back his chair and left the café. Jan picked up the carafe and refilled their coffee cups. "What an unpleasant little man," she said.

"I caught him watching my house through binoculars," Lacy said.

"I don't suppose he owns a black truck," Jan said.

Lacy shook her head. "When I saw him, he was in a blue sedan."

"A pity. He's just the type I would like for the villain."

"I met plenty of very ordinary-looking people in prison who did horrible things," Lacy said. "For a while I celled with a white-haired grandmother who had poisoned three husbands."

The sudden silence that blanketed the café made her aware that everyone in the place was staring at her. Jan leaned forward and broke the tension. "Keep talking that way and they're all going to want to see your prison tattoos," she said.

"I don't have any prison tattoos," Lacy said, her cheeks burning.

"Everyone will be so disappointed," Jan said. "When people come through a horrible experience like that, we expect them to wear their scars on the outside." She leaned forward and grasped Lacy's hand. "Don't be afraid of shocking people. Sometimes that's exactly what we need to wake us up to the real world. It's very easy to get complacent, hidden away in this little town. We start to think we're special—protected from the bad things that plague other people. We don't like it when things—like murder—happen to remind us that's not true, but sometimes it's exactly what we need. You're exactly what we need."

Chapter Nine

Lacy was still trying to figure out what Ja[r]
Selkirk had meant at Kate's that morning whe[n]
Travis called. "Do you have time today to ge[t]
together with me?" he asked. "I have som[e]
more questions for you."

"I don't know," she said. "Let me check m[y]
calendar. After all, I'm so busy these days, wha[t]
with being unemployed and losing that boxin[g]
match and all. Well, what do you know? I hav[e]
an opening."

He chuckled. "Why don't I stop by aroun[d]
lunch time?"

"Are you offering to take me to lunch? Be[-]
cause I'm going crazy sitting around the house."

"All right."

When he pulled up in his SUV a little be[-]
fore noon, Lacy was waiting on the front porc[h]
and walked out to the street to meet him. "Th[e]
bruises don't look so bad today," he said.

"You sure know how to lay on the compli[-]

ments, Sheriff." She opened the passenger door and slid in. "Thanks for agreeing to go out. My mom has been through so much, I don't want to lose my temper with her, but her hovering is driving me nuts."

"She worries about you."

"Yes, but I need a little breathing space."

"Is it okay if lunch is a picnic?" he asked. "I picked up some sandwiches and stuff from Iris Desmet."

"The Cake Walk is open again?"

"No, but she's doing some catering and stuff out of her home. I guess being idle didn't suit her any more than it does you."

"A picnic is fine," Lacy said. "In fact, it would be nice to eat without everyone in the restaurant watching me. I'm beginning to feel a little bit like the local freak on display."

"People are curious, but it will pass," he said. "But it suits me if we skip the restaurant today. Your mother and my office manager aren't the only people in town who are interested in what we have to say to each other. And it's never a good idea to discuss a case in public. You never know who might overhear something they shouldn't."

"I don't think I was prepared for all the attention I'm attracting," she said. "I was in Kate's this morning and said something about being in prison and you would have thought I had confessed to kicking small children for fun."

"They'll get over it," he said.

"I guess that curiosity is what sells books like the one Alvin Exeter is writing," she said. "By the way, he came by Kate's this morning and tried to interview Jan Selkirk. She shut him down."

"Jan is quite a formidable woman. One of her last acts as mayor was to invite—or rather insist—that I present a report to the town council. She wanted to know what the youngest sheriff the county had ever had was planning for their community. It was like standing for inspection with an army drill sergeant. I thought she would send me away if I had a scuff on my boots or a spot on my tie."

"She told me I was what the town needed, to remind them they aren't as special and safe as people think they are here." She stared out the window, at the passing vista of mountains and wildflowers. "I was kind of hoping it *would* be special and safe here."

"I guess if that was really true, I wouldn't have a job," he said. "Though I would just as soon stick to helping lost tourists and chasing off the occasional shoplifter."

"You'd be bored silly if that was the case," she said. "Admit it—you like the adrenaline rush of going after the bad guys. You wouldn't be a cop if that wasn't true."

His hands tightened on the steering wheel. "All right. Maybe some of that is true."

"It's okay," she said. "I don't hold it against you." She could even say she admired that about him—his determination to right wrongs. Though that aspect of his character had helped put her in jail, it had also made him work tirelessly until she was free. Another man might not have been so willing to admit he had made a mistake.

He headed over the bridge out of town, to a picnic area on a small lake with a view of Mount Rayford. "I remember coming here for a cookout with the senior class of Eagle Mountain High," she said as she helped him carry their lunch to one of the concrete tables. They had the place to themselves and settled in the shade of the canopy over the table.

"A local tradition," he said. "The year of our picnic it rained. You'd be surprised how many teenagers you can fit under one of these canopies."

"That all seems so long ago," she said. She had been a different person then, one who had thought the bad things of the world would never touch her.

"They still do those senior picnics," Travis

said as he laid out their own meal. "One of the advantages of a smaller school—you're able to keep up traditions like that."

"It's nice to know some things haven't changed," she said. "I was only away three years and there's so many things I don't recognize—new people and businesses. And this Pioneer Days Festival—that's new."

"Some people thought Jan was crazy to suggest it," he said. "But it's been a big success. It's a real boost for local business. Though I'll admit, it keeps our department busy. Nothing big, but you bring a lot of people in from other places and crowd them all together, and you're bound to see an uptick in petty crime—shoplifting, public drunkenness, minor things like that."

"At least you're not up to your ears in serious crimes," she said. She bit into a ham sandwich.

"I went out to see Henry Hake this morning," he said, reminding her of the one very serious crime he was investigating. "He says he got some threatening letters from people who didn't want the resort project to go forward and Andy was looking into them."

Lacy set down the sandwich. A chill shuddered through her in spite of the warm day. "So whoever wrote the letters might have killed Andy to stop him?"

"Maybe. Did Andy mention anything like that to you?"

"No," she said. "What did the letters say?"

"I don't know. Hake said he destroyed them. But they frightened him enough that he hired a bodyguard for a while."

"The only people I know who were against the development were the Utes and Paige Riddell's environmental group. But they weren't subtle about their objections to the development—they went after Hake directly—in court. And they won."

"And Hake says after they won—well, after Andy died—the threats stopped. And the development never did go forward."

"That surprises me," Lacy said. "From what I remember, they had sunk a lot of money into the project."

"He says they're restructuring—'they' being him and some partners he insists want to remain silent." He took a bite of sandwich and chewed.

"I wonder if the partners know any more about the source of the threats?" Lacy asked.

"I'm going to see if the district attorney can subpoena him for the names," Travis said. "But that will take a while, and Hake says some of the original partners are dead."

"And that makes me wonder how they died."

She plucked a grape from the bunch he had set in the middle of the table. "Then again, maybe I read too many murder mysteries. The prison library was full of them."

"I like that you don't mind talking about it," he said. "Especially around me."

"I can't pretend it never happened." She crunched down on the grape. "Later, I hope I don't think about it so much, but I'm still too close to it. I still wake up in the morning thinking I'm back there. I've missed head count and I'm going to lose my exercise privileges, or access to the commissary, or any one of a dozen punishments they can mete out for the slightest infraction."

He nodded, his mouth tight, the lines around his eyes deepening.

"I'm not telling you this to make you feel bad," she said.

"Why are you telling me, then?"

She considered the question, a warmth blossoming in her chest as the answer came to her. "Because I want you to know me," she said softly. "And that's part of me."

He slid his hand across the table and took hers, his fingers warm and slightly rough against hers. They sat that way for a long moment, holding on to something precious, neither wanting to break the spell.

A gray jay circled overhead, screeching at them in a bid for part of their lunch. Lacy pulled away and straightened, suddenly self-conscious. "I shouldn't keep you from your work," she said. "And my mother will be wondering where I've gotten to."

"I was hoping you'd have time to go through that second file box this afternoon," he said. "I want to see if we can find anything more about these threats of Hake's silent partners."

"As I said before, my afternoon just happens to be free."

TRAVIS FELT WARMED by more than the sun as he drove Lacy back to her house. There in the park, he had felt her truly softening toward him. When she talked about her time in prison, she didn't come across as someone who had been scarred by the experience. He would give her back those lost years, if there was any way possible, but at least he could let go of the feeling that he had ruined her life.

In the Milligans' dining room, they opened the second file box and each took half the papers. This box contained mostly legal documents—the deeds for the various mining claims that made up the proposed resort, copies of surveys, title searches, newspaper articles about the project and dense legal contracts relating to everything from water and mineral rights to public right of way on historic trails. After an hour, Travis tossed aside a sheaf of papers and rubbed his eyes. "I think I've found a cure for insomnia," he said.

Lacy laughed. "It does get a little dense at times," she said. "One reason I'd never want to be a lawyer."

"Have you found anything interesting?" he asked.

She shook her head. "Not a thing."

She stretched her arms over her head, a gesture that lifted her breasts and made his mouth go dry. He looked away and cleared his throat. "Maybe we'll find something in the other boxes."

"Let's go out there now," she said. "That is, if you have time."

"Let me check in with the office and see."

Adelaide reported that the office was "as dead as Methuselah's cat," and Travis wondered if she lay awake nights trying to come up with colorful expressions to add to her repertoire. "I'm going to make a run out to Andy Stenson's storage facility to look at some more files," he said. "Call me if anything pops up."

"Who else would I call?" Adelaide said breezily. "Say hello to Lacy for me."

"How did you know I'm with Lacy?"

"Your SUV is parked in front of her house. If you really want to sneak around, you're going to have to learn to be more subtle."

"I am not sneaking a—" But Adelaide had already hung up.

Lacy said goodbye to her parents and she and Travis headed out the door. They were almost to his vehicle when Alvin Exeter stepped out from his car, which was parked across the street, and held a cell phone to his eye.

Lacy froze. "Did you just take our picture?" she asked.

Alvin grinned. "You two make a handsome couple—or you will when those bruises heal." He studied the screen of his camera. "This makes a more touching image, I think. The victim and the lawman."

"You're on thin ice, Exeter," Travis said, barely controlling his anger. "I've warned you about harassing Ms. Milligan."

"I'm standing in a public street and so are you. I know my rights as a writer."

Lacy took Travis's arm. "Come on, let's go," she said.

Travis held the passenger door for her, then went around the driver's side. Exeter watched, smirking and taking picture after picture with his camera. "I'd like to rip that phone out of his hand and stomp on it," Travis said.

"He gets a charge out of being confrontational," she said. "The best way to deal with someone like him is to ignore them."

Travis glanced at her. "You're pretty smart for someone so young."

"I keep telling myself the old children's rhyme still holds true," she said. "Sticks and stones may break my bones but words can never harm me."

He pulled into the street and headed for Main. "Words can do plenty of harm and we both know it," he said when they had left Exeter behind.

"Only if I let them," she said. "Being in prison was hard, but it taught me that I need to be my own best friend. I can't really rely on anyone else."

"You can rely on me," he said.

He could feel her eyes on him, though he kept his gaze on the road. "Yes, I'm beginning to believe that," she said.

They were both silent until he turned onto Fireline Road. A dusty brown Jeep blew past them and sped onto the highway.

"I think that was Ian Barnes," Lacy said, looking over her shoulder at the dust that hung in the wake of the Jeep's passing. "Jan said he drove an old Jeep. What was he doing out here?"

"There are some rock cliffs out this way

that are popular with climbers," Travis said. "Maybe he was checking them out."

Lacy faced forward once more. "What do you know about him?" she asked.

"Not much. I met him at Eagle Mountain Outfitters. I think he's a friend of the owners. Wade Tomlinson told me he's an Iraq and Afghanistan veteran and suffers from PTSD. Why?"

She shrugged. "I don't know. There's just something about him I find…unsettling. Maybe it's the way he watches me."

"Maybe he's trying to work up the nerve to ask you out." His throat felt tight as he said the words.

"Hah! Trust me, the way the women around here are always ogling him, he could get a date with any one of them. He doesn't need me."

"But maybe you're the one he's attracted to."

"Right." She brushed a lock of hair off her face. "Because I'm so attractive with two black eyes, a busted lip and a row of stitches across my head. Though maybe he's into zombie chic."

"So you don't go for the chiseled look?" he asked, keeping his voice light.

"Chiseled is right. He looked like someone carved him from granite."

"I wouldn't want to meet him in a dark alley.

He looks like he could take me apart with his bare hands."

"You look like you could hold your own in a fight, Sheriff."

The air between them felt suddenly charged. "Are you saying you've been checking me out?" he asked.

"I've been locked up with nine hundred other women for three years," she said. "I check out every man I meet." But her smile seemed to say that she liked what she had seen when she looked at him. He had to fight the urge not to puff out his chest.

He stopped at the entrance to the storage facility and punched in the code Brenda had given him. The barrier rose and he drove to the first row of units on the right and parked. "I don't see anyone else out here," Lacy said as she and Travis climbed out of his SUV.

"I checked and only about half the units are rented," Travis said as he fitted the key into the padlock on the Stensons' unit. "Tom Reynolds owns the place and he told me most of the time people stash their stuff out here and don't look at it for years. The payment comes out of their bank account automatically every month and they probably never even think about the boxes of old clothes and papers or Grandma's furniture or whatever it is they're paying to store."

He shoved up the rolling metal door and it rose with a groan. Everything looked exactly as he had left it when he was here with Brenda, boxes and furniture piled haphazardly, everything smelling of dust and old paper. "Let me get the video recorder set up before you go in," Travis said. "We might as well do all this by the book."

Lacy waited while he set up the recorder on its tripod, then she moved into the unit ahead of him. "Where do we start?" she asked.

"The boxes are labeled alphabetically," Travis said. "Why don't you glance through a couple and see if anything catches your eye." He lifted a box from a stack and set it on top of Andy's desk. "And look for any *H*'s. The boxes we looked at already were labeled Hake, but maybe some papers related to the development ended up mixed in with the general files."

"All right." Lacy accepted the box he slid toward her and began flipping through the papers. Every few seconds she would pull up a file folder and examine it more closely. The sun beat down on the metal building and even with the door open, it grew stifling.

Lacy stopped to wipe sweat from her forehead. "Maybe we should just grab a couple and take them back to the house," she said.

"Good idea," Travis said. "Let me get my

tape from the SUV and we'll seal up a couple to go through later."

He turned and had taken two steps toward the door when an explosion ripped through the air and knocked him to the ground.

Chapter Ten

The concussion from the blast slammed Lacy to the concrete floor of the storage unit and sent a tower of boxes tumbling over her. She lay stunned, head spinning, trying to make sense of the roaring in her ears and the pain in her knees and hands.

"Lacy!" Travis's voice rose above the roar.

She lifted her head. "I'm here!" she cried, the sound weak and barely audible even to her own ears. She took a deep breath, inhaling smoke, and coughed violently, then tried again. "Here!" she shouted, hoarse.

"Can you move?" Travis shouted. "Head toward my voice."

She rose up on her knees and shoved boxes and papers away from her. Then she felt the heat of the fire licking at her back. Terror sent her lunging forward, fighting against a wall of boxes and scattered furniture. "Help!" she shouted. "Help me!"

"I'm coming!" The wall of debris shifted, and a hand reached in, groping wildly for her.

Lacy took the hand and was yanked forward, half carried toward a blast of fresh air. Then she and Travis were rolling in the gravel, his hands beating at her back, and the flames that licked there. Then he pulled her to her feet and they ran, away from the burning storage unit, into the field beyond, where they collapsed, arms still tightly wrapped around each other. Even there, the tower of flame that reached toward the sky radiated heat over them.

Lacy's eyes filled with tears as she looked into his soot-streaked face. His eyes met hers, and he rested the back of his hand to her cheek. "I thought I'd lost you," he whispered.

She took his face in both hands and pressed her lips to his, the kiss desperate in its intensity. He wrapped both arms around her and rolled onto his back, carrying her with him, their lips still locked together, her body stretched atop his. Tears ran down her face and mixed with the soot. She tasted the salt of them as she opened her mouth to deepen the kiss. Everything—the roar of the fire, the ache in her knees, the stench of the smoke—receded, burned away by passion. Some part of her, banked and given up for dead all these years, roared to life, fueled by the feel of his hard, male body beneath her.

by his searching lips and caressing hands. She wanted. She needed. She took.

He was the first to pull away, breaking the kiss and rolling her aside, then sitting up and taking both her hands in his. "I need to call this in," he said.

She nodded, unable to speak, adrenaline still pumping through her body. He released her hands, only to caress her cheek again. "You're the most amazing woman," he said.

"You're making a habit of saving my life," she said.

His expression hardened and he dropped his hand. "You don't owe me anything."

"This isn't about debts and payments," she said.

"Then what is it about?"

"It's about you making me feel more alive than I have in years. It's about… I don't know." She looked away. She had almost said "love," but that was absurd.

"Maybe it doesn't matter why right now," he said. He pulled her close again, so that her head rested on his shoulder. "I'm just glad you're okay. That we're both okay."

She turned her head to watch the fire. Other storage units had caught now, their contents feeding the blaze into even more of an inferno. "I heard an explosion," she said.

He nodded and, with one arm still wrapped around her, shifted to take out his phone. "This is Rayford County Sheriff Travis Walker. The storage units at the end of Fireline Road are burning. There was an explosion. We need the fire crew, an ambulance and a crime scene team out here." He listened a moment. "Just some burns. No fatalities. Get an officer out here to block the road," he said. "I don't want anyone back here but emergency personnel."

He ended the call and replaced his phone on his belt. "Why do we need an ambulance?" she asked.

"You've got blood on your hands, and you might have some burns." He took her wrist and turned her palm up to reveal the drying blood there.

"I scraped my hands and knees on the concrete when the blast threw me down," she said. "What about you? Are you hurt?"

He shook his head. "I was closer to the door, so the blast threw me forward." He squinted toward the blaze, black smoke billowing to the sky. "My SUV is probably on fire by now. And all of Andy's files."

"Do you think that's why this happened?" she asked. "So that we couldn't get to those files?"

"That would be my guess. I know one thing—

I want to talk to Ian Barnes and find out what he was doing out here."

"Do you think he booby-trapped the storage unit or something?"

"Or something," Travis said. "Maybe he was just checking out places to climb, but he might have seen someone else out here."

Sirens sounded in the distance. Travis shoved to his feet, then offered her his hand and pulled her up beside him. "Sounds like the cavalry is on the way," he said. "Let's see if we can circle around to the road and meet them."

Lacy kept her hand in his as they hiked over the rough ground, around the still-raging blaze and out to the road. She had kissed him in an adrenaline rush of fear and elation, but she didn't regret the impetuous gesture. Danger hadn't changed her feelings for Travis, but it had made her see the foolishness of playing hide-and-seek with her emotions. Crazy as it seemed on the surface, the man who had been her worst enemy was fast becoming her best friend.

THE FRONT PAGE of the *Eagle Mountain Examiner* had a three-column color photo of the fire at the storage units, with a smaller inset picture of Travis and Lacy, scorched and ragged, standing surrounded by half a dozen emergency personnel. "You look like two extras in a low-budget horror film," Adelaide said as she laid the paper on Travis's desk.

Travis scowled at the photo. "I didn't even know this was taken."

"Tammy was at Kate's this morning, crowing about getting the story in just under deadline," Adelaide said. "You bumped a piece about the Eighth Grade Science Fair. She had to move the pictures of Olivia Dexter's first-place exhibit on DNA testing to page four."

"My apologies to Olivia," he said. "Have we heard anything from the arson examiner?"

"He says you're keeping him busy," Adelaide said. "He sent over his preliminary findings this morning—it was definitely a bomb, with some kind of trip mechanism, probably set to go off on a delay once someone triggered it."

"Adelaide, you aren't supposed to read official reports addressed to me."

"He sent it to the general office email and I'm in charge of the general office." She waited while he logged on to his computer and opened the email from the county's arson investigator. "You know, I think I read terrorists use those kind of bombs over in Iraq and Afghanistan," she said. "That way they can make sure all our soldiers are inside a building before they blow them all up."

"Go back to work, Adelaide," Travis said. "And close the door behind you."

He read the investigator's report, though everything was as Adelaide had said. The bomb wasn't sophisticated, but it was effective, and the kind of thing anyone with a rudimentary knowledge of explosives could use. He closed the file and left his office.

"Where are you going?" Adelaide asked as he passed her desk.

"Out."

He drove instead of walked, wanting the security of a vehicle around him. His SUV had been consumed in the blaze, so he was using the department's "spare" vehicle, an ancient 4Runner with a dented door, sagging seats and no air-conditioning. He would have to petition the county commissioners for funds for a new vehicle and probably wait for an insurance settlement to come through before he could get a new ride.

He parked in front of Eagle Mountain Outfitters and went inside. Wade looked up from the cash register, an outdoor magazine open on the counter in front of him. "Hey, Sheriff, what can we do for you?" he asked.

"I'm looking for your friend Ian," Travis said.

"He isn't here."

"Where is he?" Travis asked.

"Is something wrong, Sheriff?" Wade asked.

"I need to speak to Barnes. Where is he?"

"He's staying over at the Bear's Den," Wade said. "Paige Riddell's place. Why do you need to see Ian?"

"I just want to talk to him." Before Wade could question him further, Travis left the store, got back in his vehicle and drove three blocks to Paige Riddell's Bear's Den Inn. The faded brown Jeep he and Lacy had seen turning off Fireline Road yesterday sat in the driveway of the two-story Victorian home, next to Paige's red Prius. Paige answered when he rang the doorbell. She was a tall woman, with straight, shoulder-length, honey-blond hair and serious gray eyes. In addition to operating the bed-and-breakfast, she taught yoga at the local gym and headed up Eagle Mountain Conservationists, the environmental group that had succeeded in getting an injunction to stop Henry Hake's resort development. "Sheriff Walker," she said. "What can I do for you?"

"I need to talk to one of your guests—Ian Barnes."

Her eyes narrowed. "What about?"

"That's none of your business and you know it, Paige. Can I come in?"

She opened the door wider and let him walk

past. "Ian is uncomfortable with strangers," she said. "He suffered horribly in the war."

Travis turned to study her. In her midthirties, and a little too serious for his tastes, but she might appeal to a man like Barnes. "You and he are friends?"

"No. But I respect his privacy."

"So do I. Which is why I won't tell you what this about. Is he here?"

"He's upstairs, in the sunroom off the back of the house." She nodded toward a set of carpeted stairs.

Travis took the stairs quickly, but Ian met him at the top. The muscular veteran in the black knit cap filled the doorway to the sunroom, his expression blank. "Sheriff," he said, no inflection to the word.

"Let's go into the sunroom where we can talk in private," Travis said.

Barnes backed into the room, keeping his gaze fixed on Travis. He sat in a square, heavy wood rocker in the back corner of the room. Travis pulled up a wrought-iron armchair. "I saw you out on Fireline Road yesterday afternoon," he said. "What were you doing out there?"

"I was looking for places to climb. I heard there were some good routes up Dakota Ridge back that way."

"Did you go by the storage units at the end of the road? Maybe turn around there, or stop and take a look around?"

"No." His expression and his voice never changed, both as cold as a robot's. In Travis's experience, being interviewed by the police made most people a little nervous, even if they were innocent of any wrongdoing. The first time he had interviewed Lacy after Andy's murder, she had fidgeted constantly, and practically vibrated with tension. At the time, he had mistaken her unease for a sign of guilt.

Ian Barnes might have been talking to a store clerk or a complete stranger, for all the emotion he displayed. Was he that unfeeling—or simply more experienced at dealing with law enforcement? "You know about the bomb that went off out at the storage units yesterday afternoon," Travis said.

"I saw the paper."

"But you don't know anything about it."

"No."

"Someone suggested to me that this might have been the type of bomb used by terrorists in Iraq and Afghanistan, with a delayed timer. You must have run into that sort of device while you were serving over there."

"Yes."

"So you would know how to put one together. How to deploy it."

"I know a lot of things. Yesterday I was looking for places to climb. I don't know anything about your bomb." He stood, an imposing figure looming over Travis. It was hard not to read the gesture as an intentional threat.

Travis rose also, and found that he and Barnes were almost the same height. He looked the other man in the eye. "Why are you in Eagle Mountain, Mr. Barnes?" he asked.

"I'm visiting friends. Doing some climbing."

"Have you been to the area before?"

Something flickered in those impassive brown eyes, a shadow of something—guilt? Fear? "No."

Travis knew he was lying. All his words thus far might have been lies, but Travis was certain about this one. Ian could have said he had visited Wade and Brock before, or come here on vacation. Instead, he had lied. Why?

"If you had something to do with this, I'll find out," he said. He turned to leave, but at the door, Ian's words stopped him.

"If you want to know who has it in for you and your girlfriend, you should talk to that writer, Exeter," he said.

Travis turned to face Ian again. He could have protested that Lacy wasn't his girlfriend, but the memory of her in his arms after the fire cast doubt on the truth of that statement. "Why Exeter?" he asked instead.

"He was in Moe's Pub the other night, mouthing off about the power of the written word and making Lacy pay for being so rude to him."

"What did he say, exactly?" Travis asked.

Ian sat in the rocker again and picked up a book from the table beside it. "Ask him," he said, then opened the book, ignoring Travis.

Paige met Travis at the bottom of the stairs. "Did you upset him?" she asked.

"Do you really think anything upsets him?" Travis asked.

"Not everyone wears his feelings on his sleeve," she said. "Some are more stoic."

Travis headed for the door, then thought better of it and faced her again. "When that environmental group you head was opposing Henry Hake's resort development, did any of your members do more than protest?"

She wrinkled her forehead. "What do you mean? We filed an injunction against him in court and we won. We succeeded in stopping the development—which was a ridiculous idea, anyway. The environment at those elevations is far too delicate to support the kind of infrastructure Hake wanted to build—all so a few ultrarich people could enjoy looking down on the rest of us from their ridiculously oversize homes."

"Did you write threatening letters to him? Destroy equipment?"

Her eyes widened. "No! Our group doesn't just work for the environment—we're committed to peace. It's part of our core values and mission statement."

"But you don't control all your members," he said. "Maybe one of them stepped out of line."

"Not that I'm aware of."

Travis glanced up the stairs, wondering if Barnes was listening. "Someone threatened Henry Hake back then. Someone destroyed machinery on his property. Andy Stenson was looking into those threats. It may have been what got him killed."

Paige looked pained. "I don't know anything about that," she said. "It's horrible to even think about."

"Think about it," Travis said. "And maybe ask your guest upstairs how many men he's killed."

He left, shutting the door a little harder than necessary behind him. Maybe his last words had been a low blow. He hadn't meant to frighten Paige, only to warn her about the kind of man she might be harboring. Travis couldn't see how Ian Barnes had had anything to do with Andy Stenson, but his presence out on Fireline Road yesterday had to be more than coincidence. And when Travis looked into Barnes's eyes, he saw a man with no conscience. A man like that might do anything.

Chapter Eleven

Lacy stared at the check in her hand, at the machine-printed numbers—210,000 dollars. More money than she had ever seen in her life. "I'll have to open a bank account to deposit it," she said. She hadn't had a bank account since before she went to prison.

"Have you thought about what classes you'd like to take?" her father asked. "What career you'd like to pursue?"

She shook her head. "I don't know. I think I'd like to get a car first." Her eyes met his over the top of the check. "Nothing flashy. It doesn't even have to be new, but I'd like to be able to go places without borrowing Mom's car."

"Of course." Jeanette rubbed her daughter's shoulder. "And you have until August to decide about school. You might even be able to take some courses online at first, until you decide for sure on a major."

"Yeah. That's a good idea."

"Do you want me to take you to the bank now?" her father asked.

"Sure, Dad. That's a great idea. I'll just go upstairs and get my purse."

When she came back down, both her parents were waiting by the front door. "I think this calls for a celebration," her mother said. "Maybe a special dinner."

"Sure." Lacy forced a smile. "But maybe here at home? We could order takeout so you don't have to cook."

"I don't mind cooking," Jeanette said. "We'll stop at the grocery store after the bank. We'll keep it simple—steaks and a salad. Is there anyone you'd like to invite?"

No. Yes. "Maybe… Travis?" Was she ready for that? Dinner with her family?

Jeanette's smile widened. "That's a wonderful idea."

Lacy wanted to tell her mother not to read too much into this. Travis was a friend. A friend she had been ready to jump right there on the ground next to the burning storage units, but she could blame at least part of that reaction on the sheer euphoria of surviving the explosion, right? "He might have to work," she said.

"Why don't you call right now and ask him?" Jeanette said. "We'll wait."

She realized both her parents were prepared to stand right there while she made the call, so she turned around and retraced her steps to her room, where she pulled out her cell phone—the one her parents had had waiting for her when she first arrived home, a first real symbol of her freedom.

Travis answered on the second ring. "Lacy. Is everything okay?"

"Why wouldn't it be okay?"

"You've never called me before."

"I wanted to invite you to dinner. At my house. With my parents. We're kind of celebrating. I got my check from the state." She said everything quickly, wanting to get it all out before she lost courage.

"Tonight?"

"Yes. I told them you might have to work, but I thought I would call and—"

"I'll be there. Unless some emergency comes up."

"Great. Be here about six."

She ended the call, feeling a little giddy, and almost floated down the stairs.

"He must have said yes," her mother said as Lacy joined her parents by the door.

"What makes you say that?" Lacy did her best to act nonchalant.

"You have that look in your eye," her mother said.

"What look?"

"A very pleased-with-yourself look." She reached out and touched the ends of Lacy's hair, where it skimmed her shoulder blades. One of the women on her prison block had cut it with a pair of contraband nail scissors in exchange for cookies Lacy purchased in the prison commissary. "We could stop by Lou's Salon on the way home and see if she could work you in," she said. "Maybe shape it up a little."

Lacy started to protest that she didn't want that—then realized she did. She wasn't an inmate who didn't care about her appearance anymore. "All right," she said. "That would be nice."

She was surprised at how nervous she felt about opening a bank account, but the clerk was professional and didn't even blink when Lacy handed over the check. "Would you like to deposit a portion of this in an investment account?" she asked. "I could make an appointment for you to speak to one of our financial counselors."

"Not today," Lacy said. "But next week would be good." One step at a time.

With a pad of temporary checks tucked in her purse, Lacy left the bank and headed across the parking lot with her parents. Her mother nudged her and leaned close to whisper in her ear. "Who is that good-looking young man who is staring at you?" she asked.

Lacy looked over her shoulder, starting when she recognized Ian Barnes.

Her father, who had just unlocked the driver's door, looked over the top of the car. "I think he's friends with the two guys who run Eagle Mountain Outfitters," he said. "I went in there looking for a bite valve to replace the one on my hydration pack that's been leaking and he was there. I think he's ex Special Forces or something."

"Well, he's certainly impressive," Jeanette said. She slid into the front passenger seat and cast a sideways glance at her husband, her cheeks rosy. "Well, he is. In an overly muscular kind of way."

"I wonder how he knows the mayor?" her father asked.

Only then did Lacy realize Ian was standing with Mayor Larry Rowe. She looked back and Larry clapped the younger man on the shoulder, then walked away.

"You know Larry," her mother said. "He makes it his business to know everyone in town. A good quality in a mayor, I guess. Lacy, have you met him before?"

"The mayor?" Lacy asked, deliberately misunderstanding her mother's question.

"No—that good-looking young man."

Lacy decided it was time to change the subject. "What's this Pioneer Days Festival like?" she asked. "Have you been?"

"It's quite the production," her father said. "There's a parade and a special display at the museum. Last year Brenda and Jan dressed in 1890s swimming costumes and sold lemonade and sugar cookies. There's a stage in the park with bands and crafts vendors, a baseball game and foot races and I forget what else."

"Fireworks," her mother said. "They shoot them off above town. They do a wonderful job."

"The whole thing was Jan Selkirk's idea," her father said. "She spent two years persuading the town fathers to adopt the idea, and then was able to gloat when it turned out to be such a big success. The new mayor, Larry Rowe, and his council have expanded on her original idea and attracted quite a bit of attention to our little town."

"They keep talking about creating a similar festival for winter, when business is slow," Jeanette said. "But the weather can be so iffy then."

"A big snow and avalanches could cut off

Dakota Pass and everyone could be snowed in," George said. "The locals are used to it, but tourists might raise a fuss."

"I think it's enough having all those tourists in town for the summer," Jeanette said.

"Yes, but you're not a local businessperson," her husband countered.

Her parents continued the argument on the drive to the grocery store. Lacy sat in the back seat and let her mind drift to the place it always ended up these days—back with Travis and the kiss they had shared after the explosion. When she closed her eyes, she could still feel the scrape of the beard just beneath his skin as she pressed her cheek to his, the hard plane of his chest crushed against her breasts, the implements on his belt digging into her belly—the length of his desire confirming that he wanted her as much as she wanted him.

So what did she do? Instead of arranging to see him privately, where maybe they could see where that desire would take them, she had invited him to a family dinner, where she would be too uptight to even risk a kiss under her parents' watchful eyes. Not that her mother and father were prudes, but a new relationship— one she didn't even know how to define—required privacy.

Her father stopped and signaled for the turn

into the parking lot of Eagle Grocery. A black-and-white sheriff's department vehicle, lights flashing and sirens blaring, sped by, followed closely by a second vehicle and an ambulance.

"My goodness, what's that all about?" her mother asked.

Lacy had already dug her phone from her purse and punched in the number for the sheriff's department. Adelaide answered immediately. "What's going on?" Lacy demanded.

"I'm not allowed to give out information about sheriff's department calls over the phone," Adelaide said. "You people ought to know that by now."

"This is Lacy Milligan. Just tell me—is Travis hurt?"

The silence that followed lasted so long Lacy thought Adelaide had hung up on her. "You can't tell anyone where you heard this," Adelaide said finally, her voice lowered.

"I won't. I promise."

"We had a report of an officer down, out at the storage units on Fireline Road. We don't know that it's Travis."

"Even I know the sheriff's department doesn't have that many officers," Lacy said. "We just saw two cars go by. If Travis wasn't in either one of those…"

"I have to go now, Lacy. I have a lot of

other calls coming in. Try not to worry, but it wouldn't hurt to say a prayer."

Lacy ended the call to Adelaide and let the phone fall into her lap. "What is it, dear?" her mother asked.

Lacy swallowed, her mouth too dry to speak. *Keep it together*, she scolded herself. "There was an Officer in Distress call," she said.

"Travis?" her father asked.

"They don't know." The awfulness of those words settled over her like a smothering blanket, and it was all she could do to remain seated upright and breathing.

TRAVIS WAS AT the motel out on the highway, trying to track down Alvin Exeter, when the Officer in Distress call went out. As soon as he heard the address, he raced to his car, dialing his phone as he ran. He tried the office first, but the line was busy. No surprise there. Half the town had probably called in to see what was going on. The line was supposed to be for sheriff's department business only, but too many people knew about it and felt free to use it any time they wanted. He could have called Adelaide on the radio, but he didn't have time to waste.

He started the Toyota and hit the speed dial

for Gage. "What's up?" he asked as he sped from the parking lot.

"Travis! Thank God!" Gage almost shouted the words. "We got the Officer in Distress call from Dispatch and they didn't know what unit. Since it was out at the storage units, I thought—"

"Where's Dwight?" Travis cut off his brother's relieved babbling.

"He's right behind me."

"No one else should be on duty," Travis said.

"They aren't."

"Then who put in the call?" He eased off the gas pedal, mind racing. "Is this some kind of trap?"

"Dispatch thought it was legit. Are we gonna risk not checking it out?"

"No, we aren't. But we need to be careful."

He was closer to Fireline Road than the other two units, but it wasn't long before they fell in behind him, a wailing, flashing parade of three sheriff's department vehicles, an ambulance and one state highway patrol car. Travis wouldn't have been surprised to see the fire department and Search and Rescue trailing them.

A red Jeep Wagoneer was parked in front of the gate at the entrance to the storage units. Travis swore when he recognized the vehicle.

Gage's voice came on the radio. "Eddie," he said. "What's he doing out here?"

Eddie Carstairs was one of the reserve officers, called in when someone was out sick or on vacation, or when Travis needed extra manpower to work an accident or a festival. At twenty-two, Eddie looked about sixteen. His straight black hair flopped over a high forehead, and his face was long and droopy, which had led to the nickname Gage had saddled him with—"Hound Dog."

Travis pulled in beside Eddie's Jeep and shut off the Toyota, the engine sputtering twice in protest. From here he could make out a figure in jeans and a T-shirt, face down on the dirt a few yards from the blackened area that marked the reach of the fire. Travis pulled out his phone and called Eddie's number. "Officer Carstairs, this is Sheriff Walker. Can you hear me?"

The body on the ground didn't move.

Travis scanned the area around the body, then the hills beyond, searching for some clue as to what had happened. Gage and Dwight moved to his window, crouching down so that they were shielded between the Toyota and the Jeep. "What do you think?" Gage asked.

"What did Dispatch say about the call?" Travis asked.

"It came in on a private cell, not a police

number," Gage said. "I called the dispatcher Sally—you know her, the big blonde with the twins?" That was typical Gage. After five minutes with almost anyone, he would know their life history.

"What did she say about the call?" Travis prompted.

"She said the man on the other end sounded like he was having trouble breathing—or was in pain. All he said was 'Officer down'—and gave the address. Then he hung up or got disconnected."

Travis stared at the prone body, willing it to move. He took his binoculars from the field kit on the passenger-side floorboard and trained them on the figure.

"I think he's breathing," Dwight said.

"I think so, too," Travis said. Or was he imagining the faint rise and fall of the back? He laid aside the field glasses and looked at his two officers. "You two wearing your vests?"

They nodded in unison. "You think he was shot?" Dwight asked.

"That seems the most likely scenario."

"Could be a sniper," Gage said. "Up in the hills."

"If it is, I'm not risking him picking us off one by one," Travis said.

"If one of us could get behind one of the stor

ge buildings, we could shoot up into the hills,
naybe draw his fire," Dwight said.

"A smart shooter wouldn't fall for that," Travis said. "He'd wait until we were out in the
open, where he could get a clear shot." He considered the situation again. "Gage, do you have
he sniper rifle with you?"

"Yes. And two ARs and a shotgun, some
smoke grenades and a case of ammo." At Travis's raised eyebrows, he shrugged. "When the
call came in, I unlocked the arsenal and took
everything I could grab. You never know what
you're going to need."

"You take the sniper rifle and one of the
ARs," Travis said. "Dwight, you get one of the
ARs. I want one of you set up behind each of
he intact buildings on either side of Eddie."

"Where are you going to be?" Gage asked.

"I'm going out to get Eddie. You're going to
cover me."

Chapter Twelve

All thoughts of celebration vanished as Lacy and her parents drove home. Lacy started to suggest her dad drive out to Fireline Road to see what had happened, but quickly dismissed the idea. The officers didn't need civilians in the way. And it wasn't as if she could do anything to help. She would just have to sit at the house and wait.

She was surprised to find Jan and Brenda seated on the settee on the front porch when her dad pulled the car into the driveway. "We heard what happened," Jan said. "It's all anybody in town is talking about."

"But it might not be Travis," Brenda said, giving Lacy's arm a squeeze. "I called the dispatcher, Sally Graham, and she said the man who called didn't identify himself, but it wasn't Travis's phone number."

"Why don't we all go inside," Jeanette said. "I'll make coffee."

They all trooped inside and into the Millians' living room, which overlooked the street. Jeanette and George left the three younger women sitting on the sofa and love seat and went to make the coffee. "Alvin Exeter came by the history museum this morning," Jan said. "He wanted to talk to me and to Brenda."

"We both refused to speak with him," Brenda said. "But he didn't want to take no for an answer. He was really nasty about it, too."

"He said he's thinking of taking the approach that you really got away with murder," Jan said. "Since no one is coming forward to contest that theory, he figures it will be an even better story than the one of your wrongful conviction—the kind of thing that's sure to attract a lot of attention and boost sales."

"I don't care what he says," Lacy said. "He can say I murdered ten people and it won't make any difference to me. He's just trying to bait people into talking to him."

Brenda glanced toward the kitchen, then leaned toward Lacy, her voice low. "You might not care, but your parents will," she said. "It would hurt them so much."

Lacy nodded. "There's nothing I can do to stop him."

Jan and Brenda exchanged glances. "You could talk to him."

"No," Lacy said. "Just...no."

"Or," Brenda said. "You could find out wh[o] really murdered Andy."

"That's what Travis has been trying to do," Lacy said. And because of that, he might even now be dead. She shoved the thought away. N[o.] He would be okay. He had to be okay.

"There must be something in those files," Brenda said. "Something we forgot or over[looked."

"It doesn't matter now," Lacy said. "The file[s] are gone. Destroyed by the bomb."

"It's horrible to think it, but all this violenc[e] must mean you're getting close to finding th[e] real killer," Brenda said. "Otherwise, why g[o] to so much trouble to stop you?"

"We thought it must have something to d[o] with Hake Development, because that was An[]dy's biggest client," Lacy said. "But what i[f] that's not it at all? After all, he had lots of cli[]ents. Maybe it's something small that we aren'[t] thinking of at all."

"I still have Andy's computer," Brenda said[.] "I haven't turned it on since he died—I don'[t] even know if it still works."

Jan and Lacy stared at her. "Why didn't yo[u] say something before?" Lacy asked.

"I didn't think of it," Brenda said. "Andy kep[t]

ard copies of everything. I figured anything
nportant would be in his files."

"He probably had copies of a lot of stuff on
is computer," Lacy said, excitement growing.
And if you haven't even turned it on in years,
should be just fine."

"I promise I'll take it to Travis first thing to-
norrow," Brenda said.

"Better let him come to you," Jan said. "I
vouldn't take a chance going anywhere with
nything the killer might want."

"If Travis is okay," Lacy said.

Lacy's parents returned to the living room
vith a tray of cups and a coffeepot. "I turned
n the radio to see if we could get a news re-
ort and find out what's going on," her father
aid. "But I couldn't find anything."

"Lacy, you have Travis's phone number,
on't you?" her mother asked.

"Yes," she said. "I called him on it earlier."

"Have you tried calling him since all this
as happened?"

"Mom, he'll be too busy to talk—" She fell
ilent, heart leaping in her chest. She laughed at
er own foolishness and pulled out her phone.
he didn't care if Travis yelled at her for in-
errupting him while he worked, as long as he
nswered.

She punched in his number and waited while

the call connected and the ringer buzzed—once, twice, three times. "This is Sheriff Travis Walker. Leave a message at the beep."

She had heard the expression "crushed" before, but had never fully comprehended what it meant. She felt as if someone had dumped a truckload of bricks in the middle of her chest. She ended the call without leaving a message. "No answer," she said.

Brenda leaned over and squeezed her hand. "Don't give up hope," she said.

"I won't." Lacy took a deep breath and straightened. Three years in prison had taught her how to survive when things looked bleak—the only difference now was that so much more was at stake.

TRAVIS WAITED UNTIL Gage and Dwight were in position, then exited the Toyota. He wore a pack that contained blankets, a first-aid kit and water, and had unholstered his duty weapon and held it in his right hand. Eddie still hadn't moved, though a second check through the binoculars had revealed no pooling blood or obvious injuries. Still, he could be bleeding out from a chest wound or a gut shot and they might not be able to tell.

Gage signaled that they were ready and Travis began moving around to the west. His plan was to move far to the side, then rush in low, with Gage and Dwight laying down a screen of fire aimed at the hills within firing distance of Eddie. It wasn't the best plan in the world, but it was the only one he had right now. He could have waited for a helicopter or an armored vehicle from a neighboring department, but arranging that kind of backup could take hours, and Eddie might not have that kind of time.

He was halfway to the cover of the first storage unit, where Dwight waited, when his phone rang. He ignored it and silenced the phone. Everyone he needed to talk to was here right now and had better ways of communicating with him.

He stopped when he reached Dwight, who had been scanning the hills above the site with a pair of binoculars. "See anything?" Travis asked.

"Nothing." He lowered the glasses. "Could be our shooter is gone."

"Maybe." If he was, that meant they had lost their chance to pin him down, but it also meant it would be easier to get help for Eddie. He put his hand on Dwight's shoulder, the hard edge of the tactical vest beneath his palm. "You ready?"

"Ready."

Travis looked across at Gage, who nodded

in acknowledgment, then took a deep breath. "Okay. I'm going out there."

He ran bent over, on a zigzagging path that was supposed to make it harder for a shooter to target him. Behind him, bullets ripped from the magazines of the two ARs fired by his deputies in a deafening blast. Travis couldn't tell if anyone returned fire or not, though no rounds hit the dirt around him—and more important, none hit him.

The shooting stopped as he knelt beside Eddie. He put a hand on the younger man's back and relief left him shaking as he felt the steady rise and fall of his breath. "Eddie." He shook the body. "Eddie, wake up."

Eddie groaned. Travis knelt in front of him and shoved him over. The younger man landed heavily on his back with a groan.

The first thing he noticed was that Eddie's nose looked broken. It was definitely crooked, with blood crusting around the nostrils, purpling bruises under both eyes. More blood seeped from a gash in the middle of his forehead. That might explain why the young man was unconscious. So what had happened? Had they gone to all this trouble because Eddie was clumsy and had tripped and knocked himself out?

Then Travis saw the wound—a dark, round

hole in his shoulder, rimmed with blackish blood. He pressed on the wound and more blood seeped out, and Eddie groaned and stirred. His eyelids fluttered and he stared up at Travis. "Sheriff?" he asked hoarsely, and tried to sit up.

Travis pushed him back down. "Lie still," he said. "I'm going to call in the paramedics."

Thirty seconds later, a pair of paramedics swarmed around the wounded young man. Gage and Dwight, weapons in hand, emerged from the cover of the storage units and joined the growing crowd of law enforcement personnel who were milling around the area. "Get these people out of here," Travis said to Gage. "They could be compromising a crime scene."

"So he *was* shot," Dwight said.

"At least once, in the shoulder," Travis said. "Hit his head pretty good and broke his nose, too. That may be what knocked him out."

"What was he doing out here?" Dwight asked.

"Oh, he's going to explain all that, I promise," Travis said.

"My guess is he came out to look at the bomb site," Gage said. "He was hoping to be a hero and find something the arson investigator or the rest of us missed."

"So whoever set the bomb was *guarding* the

place?" Dwight asked. "Why? There can't be anything in those ashes worth finding."

"I don't know," Travis said. "Maybe extra insurance? They're so paranoid they don't want to leave anything to chance?"

"Nobody is that paranoid," Gage said.

"You never worked for a big corporation, did you?" Dwight asked. "Or the government—especially the military. Some of those people are majorly paranoid."

"Ian Barnes was in the military," Travis said. "Maybe he's that paranoid. We'd better find out where he was and what he was doing when Eddie was shot."

A second team of paramedics wheeled a gurney over the rough ground to Eddie and lifted him onto it. One of the original first responders joined Travis, Gage and Dwight. "The bullet is still in him, but he's stable," he said. "We'll know more when they get some X-rays but my guess is he'll be okay."

"What about the head injury and his nose?" Travis asked.

The paramedic grinned. "He said he was trying to run for cover when he tripped and hit a big rock. Broke his nose and knocked himself clean out."

"It's a miracle the shooter didn't take the opportunity to finish him off," Gage said.

"Maybe he thought he had killed him and didn't want to stick around and find out," Dwight said.

"Or maybe killing him wasn't the point," Travis said. "Maybe he was just sending a warning."

"Yeah," Gage said. "After all, Eddie wasn't in uniform. He wasn't driving a police vehicle. The shooter probably didn't know he's a cop."

Travis watched as the paramedics strapped Eddie onto the gurney and fitted an oxygen mask over his face. He waited until they had rolled him away toward the ambulance before he moved over to examine the place where he had fallen. By now most of the other law enforcement personnel had moved on, but he had no doubt that within a couple of hours everyone in the county would have heard about the reserve officer who had knocked himself out fleeing from a shooter. Hound Dog might never live that story down.

"Here's where he hit his head," Gage said, nudging a cantaloupe-sized chunk of granite with the toe of his boot.

"There's some scuff marks here, like this was where he was standing when he was hit," Dwight said, indicating an area on the edge of the scorch marks where the Stensons' storage unit had once stood.

Travis moved to stand beside him, and stared up into the hills. He pointed to clump of pinion trees about halfway up the slope. "What do you think? In there somewhere?"

Gage squinted up toward the area Travis indicated, then nodded. "Yeah, I think so. Good cover, shade, a good view of this area, a good angle to shoot, with the sun behind you or directly overhead most of the day, after it came up over that ridge there."

"About two hundred yards," Dwight said. "You'd have to have a high-powered rifle and be a good shot."

"I could make it," Gage said. "So could you. So could a lot of people."

"All right. Let's go up there and see what we can find," Travis said, and led the way up the slope.

ADELAIDE KINKAID TELEPHONED Lacy at four thirty. "Travis is fine," she said. "Though when I see him, I'm going to read him the riot act for not letting me know himself. I had to find out from Pamela Sue Windsor, over at the hospital in Junction, when she called to get Eddie Carstairs's insurance information. That fool Eddie was up there, poking around at the bomb site where he had no business being, and got himself shot."

Lacy didn't know or care who Pamela Sue Windsor or Eddie Carstairs were. "Travis is okay?" she asked, collapsing back against the sofa. Around her, her parents and Jan and Brenda broke into relieved smiles.

"He's fine," Adelaide said. "He and Gage and Dwight are still out there, investigating the scene. Eddie is fine, too. They're operating to remove the bullet and they have to set his broken nose because the fool tripped on a rock and knocked himself out while he was trying to run away. I swear, that rock is probably smarter than he is. I'll tell Travis you called when he comes in. Or maybe I'll leave him a note, since it's almost time for me to go home."

"Oh, no, don't tell him," Lacy said. "Please don't." She was embarrassed to have him know how panicked she had been at the idea of him hurt or dead. Whatever was between them felt too new—too fragile for that.

"Have it your way, dear. I have to go now. I have a few more calls to make. I think I remember that Eddie has a girlfriend over in Delta—I'll need to get in touch with her and hold her hand a little. These men have no consideration."

Lacy slipped the phone back into her pocket and realized everyone in the room was looking at her. "He's fine," she said. "It was another officer who was hurt, but he's going to be okay."

"You have to know more than that," Jan said. "We want the whole scoop. What happened?"

"I don't know." Lacy held out her hand to stave off the chorus of protests. "I really don't. Adelaide said this other officer—Eddie—was out at the storage units and someone shot him. And I guess he tripped and fell and broke his nose and knocked himself out, but I guess he was able to call for help before that." She shook her head. "That's all I know, really." And Travis was okay. She knew that—and that was really the most important fact. The only one she cared about.

"I'm glad I decided to have a yard sale instead of renting a storage unit," Jan said. "Who knew they could be so hazardous."

"I think the sooner I get Andy's computer out of my house, the better I'll feel," Brenda said. "Whatever was in those files of his, someone wanted to protect the information badly enough to try to kill me and Lacy and Travis and now this Eddie fellow."

"Maybe they did kill Andy," Lacy said.

Jan stood. "Come on. We'll go get the computer now and take it to the sheriff's office," she said.

"Maybe you should wait and have Travis or one of his deputies go with you," George said.

"I'll go with you," Lacy said.

"Lacy—" Her mother managed to freight the ne word with a wealth of worry.

"It's better than sitting around here," Lacy aid. "It will be fine. I promise." And if they imed their arrival at the sheriff's department ight, she might even run into Travis, and be ble to see for herself that he was all right.

Chapter Thirteen

"I still can't believe you're only just now men￼tioning that you had Andy's computer," Jan sai￼ as she followed Brenda and Lacy into Brenda￼ house. "You knew the sheriff was looking fc￼ any information Andy might have had."

"I simply forgot it existed," Brenda saic￼ "I was in the basement the other day, look￼ing for that box of fossils I told you my fathe￼ had given me—you remember we talked abou￼ using them in that ancient history display at th￼ museum. I pulled a big plastic storage containe￼ out from under the stairs and when I opened i￼ I realized it was full of stuff from Andy's o￼fice. I thought everything was out at the storag￼ unit, but apparently not. The computer was si￼ting right on top of everything else. I suppos￼ whoever packed the stuff up for me thougl￼ I would want it here, but I'm not sure I eve￼ knew I had it."

"If it's been safely packed away all this time

m sure it still works," Lacy said. "And com-
uter files should be easier to search than paper
nes."

"That doesn't mean there's going to be any-
hing useful on it," Jan said.

"No," Lacy agreed. "But maybe it will help."

"I'll just go down in the basement and get
out of the storage box," Brenda said, cross-
ng the kitchen to a set of stairs that led down.
You two can wait up here."

"I'll go," Jan said. "I know it's upsetting for
ou to see Andy's things."

"It was a shock, seeing them yesterday,"
Brenda said. "But I'm over that now. After
ll, it's been over three years. I'm not going to
reak down because I see an old law book that
sed to belong to him."

"Still, I'm sure I can go right to it, you've de-
cribed the location so well." Jan moved past
Brenda and Lacy to the top of the stairs. "Why
on't you open a bottle of wine for us?" she said
s she started down the stairs.

Lacy and Brenda's eyes met. "Is Jan always
his bossy?" Lacy whispered.

"Jan is the type of person who likes to be
n charge of any project," Brenda said. She
pened a kitchen cabinet and pulled out three
ll glasses. "Understanding that has helped
e get along with her at work. I think instead

of wine, we should have iced tea. I don't thin
we all want to show up at the sheriff's offic
with alcohol on our breaths."

While Brenda filled glasses with ice, Lac
descended the stairs to the basement. "Did yo
find it?" she called. She rounded the corner an
spotted Jan bent over a large blue plastic bin

Jan jerked her head up and saw Lacy, the
straightened. The contents of the bin in fror
of her were all in a jumble—as if they ha
been hurriedly pawed through. "Brenda sai
the computer was right on top," Lacy said. "Yo
shouldn't have to dig through the boxes."

Jan snapped the lid back onto the bin, the
pulled a laptop computer off the shelf next t
her. "I've been thinking," she said. "Maybe
should talk to that reporter—Alvin Exeter."

Just the mention of Alvin made Lacy's ston
ach churn. "Why would you want to do that?

"Maybe if someone appeared to coope
ate with him, he'd give up this crazy idea c
portraying you as guilty." She led the way u
the stairs. "I wouldn't tell him anything muc
about you, personally. I'd focus on the town
how much of a shock the crime was—and, c
course, how we all knew all along that yo
couldn't possibly have murdered Andy."

Lacy couldn't help but wonder where "all
these people who knew she was innocent ha

een during her trial, but she could see little oint in bringing that up now. "You're free to lk to whoever you like," she said, "but I doubt f you'll change his mind about anything. He trikes me as a generally nasty person."

Brenda met them at the top of the stairs. "I ee you found the laptop." She reached out and an handed it over.

"There are actually several bins of things rom Andy's office down there," Jan said. "I eeked in a couple of them and there are some ooks that might be worth some money if you vant to sell them. And I saw a couple of pho-ographs you might want to donate to the mu-eum. I'll come over one day and we can go hrough them, if you like."

"Sure," Brenda said. "That would be great." he set the computer on the kitchen table and anded Lacy and Jan glasses of tea. "I decided ve could wait on the wine until after we stop y the sheriff's department," she said.

"We don't have to all go see the sheriff," Jan aid. "When I leave here I'll take Lacy home, hen drop this off on the way to my house." he opened the computer. "We ought to see if his turns on, don't you think?" Before Brenda ould answer, she pressed the power button and he computer hummed to life.

"Looks like it's password protected," Lacy

said, looking over Jan's shoulder at the scree
that asked for the password. She and Jan looke
at Brenda.

"I have no idea what the password is," sh
said. "We could guess, but I really don't car
what's on there. I prefer to leave the snoopin;
to the police."

"But snooping can be so fun," Jan teased
But she shut down the computer and closed th
lid. "You'll feel better—and so will I—whe
you have this thing out of your house. Hope
fully, whoever was out to destroy those file
doesn't know yet that you have it."

Brenda froze, the glass of tea halfway to he
lips. "How could they? I didn't even know my
self until yesterday."

"One of the movers who helped clean ou
Andy's office might have remembered it," Ja
said. She finished off her tea, then set down th
glass and picked up the computer. "But proba
bly not. Come on, Lacy. Let's take care of this
It's early enough, maybe you and Travis car
have dinner together after all."

"How did you know about that?" Lacy asked

"Your mother told me while you were in
the bathroom," Jan said. She grinned. "I can'
help it if I have a talent for finding out thing
about people. You'd be surprised how usefu
it can be."

She started toward the living room and the others followed. They were almost to the door when the bell rang. Brenda hurried forward to answer it.

Travis's uniform was streaked with soot and something dark that might have been blood. He had more soot smudged on one cheek and his nose, and he needed a shave, but Lacy had never seen a more welcome sight. She wanted to rush forward and throw her arms around him, but she held back, hovering behind Brenda as her friend ushered the sheriff inside.

He looked past the other two women and found Lacy, his eyes meeting hers. "Your mother told me I'd find you here," he said.

"I'm glad you're okay," she said.

"Sorry if I worried you," he said. "The dispatcher didn't know the name of the officer who called in, and people jumped to conclusions. By the time I got back to the station half the town thought I was the officer who had been wounded and the other half were ready to start planning my funeral."

"I'm sorry about the officer who was shot," Lacy said. "Is he going to be okay?"

"He will be."

"Do you know who shot him?" Jan asked.

"No." Travis was still watching Lacy. "I

stopped by to see if you'd still like to have dinner with me."

"Um, sure." She was so aware of the other two women watching. She tried hard to appear casual and indifferent.

"Good." He looked down at the floor and for a long moment, no one said anything.

"Oh, really, go on, you two," Jan said. "It's at times like these that I'm reminded that the saying 'three's a crowd' is so true."

"But before you go." Brenda reached over and tugged the computer from Jan's grasp. "We were going to bring this to your office, but you can take it with you."

"A laptop?" Travis examined the computer.

"It was Andy's," Brenda said. "I didn't even realize I had it until I was looking for something in the basement and found it in a box of books and other stuff from his office. It's password protected and I don't know the password, but I thought maybe the sheriff's department could get past that. So many things, like notes and letters and photographs, Andy kept in his files, but contracts and correspondence will probably be on there. Maybe you'll find something to help you."

"This is great," Travis said. "We'll find someone to get the information off it. Thank you, Brenda."

"I'm sorry I didn't think of it before," she said.

"Are you ready to go, Lacy?" he asked.

"I'm ready."

She followed him out the door and down the walkway, aware of the other two women watching them. "This is the oldest vehicle in our little fleet," he said as he opened the passenger door of the Toyota. "It's pretty rough."

"It doesn't matter," she said, sliding into the seat. She watched as he tucked the computer into a large plastic bag, filled out a label on the front of the bag, then sealed it. He laid the bag with the computer in it on the rear floorboard. "We'll put that in an evidence locker at the station." He looked up and his eye caught hers. "Later."

"Mom was thrilled you accepted her invitation to dinner," Lacy said, as he turned onto Main. "I was, too, of course. I thought maybe you would be too tired or too busy or…"

He put his hand over hers and she stopped talking. "It's okay," he said. "You don't have to be nervous."

"I'm not sure why I am," she said. She watched him through half-lowered lashes, not wanting him to look into her eyes and see the powerful desire and attraction that had her feeling a little out of control.

He laced his fingers with hers. "I told your

mother I needed to take a rain check on the family dinner," he said. "I wanted some time for the two of us to be alone."

Lacy swallowed, her heart beating faster. "Oh."

"Is that okay with you?"

"Yes." She looked into his eyes. "More than okay."

He kissed the back of her hand, then turned it over and kissed her palm, and she suddenly felt hot and a little light-headed. "Where are we going for dinner?" she asked.

"How about my place?"

"Yes."

They held hands on the drive to the condo he rented in a development on the river. He retrieved the computer in its evidence bag from the Toyota and carried it inside, where he locked it inside a cabinet by the door. When he straightened, Lacy didn't hesitate, but moved into his arms.

The kiss was urgent, a little rough, his unshaven chin abrading her cheek, his lips crushing the still-healing cut on her mouth. But sheer pleasure overwhelmed the discomfort, and she angled her head to deepen the contact, reveling in the heat and strength of him. She wrapped her arms around him, pressing herself fully to him, and he slid his hands down to cup her bot-

om and draw her tight against him, leaving no
doubt how much he wanted her.

When he finally lifted his head and looked
into her eyes, she was shaky, her heart pounding. "Wow," she said.

"About dinner—" he began.

She wriggled against him. "I'm thinking
maybe we should enjoy dessert first."

She whooped as he lifted her, his hands under
her thighs, wrapping her legs around his waist.
He kissed her again, bracing her back against
the wall in the foyer. She squirmed, delighted
at the way he groaned in response—then she
was the one groaning as he brought one hand
up to caress the side of her breast, and began
tracing a series of warm, wet kisses along the
line of her jaw.

She tugged at his shirt, frustrated by the
equipment that jangled and poked from the belt
at his waist. Even when she succeeded in undo-
ing the top two buttons, she was blocked from
further exploration by the hard black wall of
his bulletproof vest. By this time he had her T-
shirt pushed up under her arms and was trailing
his tongue along the lace at the top of her bra.

"This isn't fair," she protested. "You're wearing too much stuff."

He raised his head and laughed, then wrapped
his hands around her waist and gently lowered

her to the floor. "Am I rushing things?" he asked, looking into her eyes.

"More like going too slow." She pulled his head down to kiss him again, then nipped his upper lip. "You're welcome to get naked right here and take me up against the wall, but don't you think a bed might be more comfortable?"

She whooped again as he picked her up once more, this time scooping her up behind her knees and shoulders. He carried her down a short hallway to a large bedroom. She had a passing impression of dark furniture and a king-size bed before he dropped her onto the mattress.

She propped herself on her elbows and watched as he stripped off his utility belt and draped it on the arm of a chair next to the bed. He kicked off his boots, then finished unbuttoning the shirt and removed it. This was the kind of male body she could admire—masculine but not too hard, handsome but not too perfect.

There was nothing particularly sexy about the black protective vest he wore under the shirt—except that he was wearing it. He peeled it off, his skin damp in places beneath it. "I should take a shower," he said.

"Only if you take me with you," she said. His eyes met hers and she felt the force of the look deep inside, a tugging heat that settled between her legs. He finished undressing, then pulled her up from the bed. When she was standing beside him she pulled her T-shirt off over her head. Before she could remove her bra, he had unfastened it and was tracing his tongue around one nipple, and then the next, until she was swaying, her kneecaps having apparently melted in the onslaught.

Some time after that the rest of her clothes ended up somewhere on the bedroom floor, and the two of them tumbled into the shower, where warm water rushed over them, and she discovered how sensual the feel of soapsuds between two naked bodies could be.

She slid soapy fingers over the jut of his shoulders and the swell of his biceps, tracing the ridges of his ribs and smoothing across the flat plane of his stomach. When she wrapped her hand around his erection, he let out his breath and his eyes glazed.

He curled a hand around her wrist. "Better slow down," he said.

She smiled up at him. "I don't know," she said. "I kind of like having you at my mercy."

"Is that so?" His grin held a hint of wickedness that sent another thrill through her. The grin gave way to a slack-jawed sigh as he reached down and slid a finger into her, stroking gently. "Now...now who needs to go...

slow," she stammered as he slid the finger in and out. "Remember...it's been a while for me."

With his free hand, he reached over and shut off the water, then kissed her again, their lips remaining locked together even as they moved out of the shower and wrapped themselves in towels.

They were still damp when they returned to the bed and tumbled onto the dark blue comforter. She scooted back onto the pillows and beckoned him to her. "I don't want to wait any longer," she said.

He leaned over and took a condom from the drawer of the bedside table. "Just so you don't get the wrong impression, these have been in there awhile," he said, holding up the foil packet. "But I think they're still good."

"Stop talking and put that baby on," she said.

"Yes, ma'am."

Watching him roll on that condom was enough to have her breathing hard again. When he finally moved over her she was more than ready for him, pulling her to him and sighing with happiness as he entered her.

She had expected a lot from this moment— physical satisfaction, a kind of completion, the thrill of being so close to him. But she hadn't counted on his gentleness, or how much he would *care* for her. He moved slowly at first his eyes locked to hers, his focus entirely on her. He shifted slightly, and she felt the movement deep inside her. "Do you like that?" he asked.

"Yes."

"How about this?" He reached down to fondle her and her eyes lost focus. *Yeesss.* His hands and his hips worked a kind of magic over her, and she surrendered to it. "That's it," he whispered, his fingers caressing a sensitive place she hadn't even known existed. "Don't be afraid to let go."

So she let go, and rode the waves of pleasure each thrust of his body sent through her. She dug her fingers into his back and responded to his every movement, opening her eyes when she felt him still and tense, watching his release reflected on his face, then pulling him to her to hold him even closer, until they rolled to the side, still joined, to gaze into each other's eyes.

"To quote you—wow," he said, and he slid out of her. He disposed of the condom in the trash basket next to the bed, then lay back down beside her.

She laughed, feeling impossibly light, as if she might float off the bed. "Yeah—wow." She trailed one finger down his nose. "Now you're making me think I missed out in high school, not flirting with you."

"I like to think I've learned a few things since high school."

"Life has a way of doing that—teaching us things whether we want to learn them or not. You taught me that people can change— or at least, they can change their minds. You changed your mind about me. And I changed my mind about you."

He slid over to lay his head on her shoulder. "Let's put that behind us," he said. "I want to focus on our future, not our past."

"Except we can't really put the past behind us," she said. "Not until we find Andy's killer— or whoever it is who keeps coming after us."

"You're right," he said. "We're going to stop them."

She eased him off her and sat up. "Why don't we start by taking a look at that laptop?" she said.

"What good will that do?" Travis asked. "Brenda said it's password protected."

"Yes, but I think I know the password. It's probably the same one Andy used for everything. That's what most people do, isn't it?"

The look he gave her held frank admiration. "I was right when I said you'd be the key to solving this case," he said.

"We haven't solved anything yet," she reminded him.

"No, but we will. And soon. I can feel it."
He slid off the bed and took her hand. "Let's
go check that laptop."

Chapter Fourteen

Travis couldn't stop looking at Lacy. He liked watching her when she was like this—completely relaxed and happy, her attention focused on the computer that was open on the coffee table between them. They sat on the sofa in his living room, thighs touching. She had put on one of his dress shirts, the cuffs folded back, the tails hanging down to midthigh. He had pulled on a pair of jeans. Just as well he didn't have the video camera here to film this, though he had made her sign off on the custody sheet, keeping to proper procedure.

"Andy's password for most things was brenda812," Lacy said as she typed. "They were married in August of 2012." She hit Enter and the screen shifted to reveal the desktop menu. "Eureka!" she cried, and clicked on a folder labeled Office.

A list of file names filled the screen. Travis leaned in closer. "Do you see anything?" he asked.

She highlighted the file named "Eagle_mtn_resort." The first thing that came up was a report from the county road commissioner. "It's about the roads in and around the resort," she said, scanning the page. "That doesn't look too pertinent."

She started to close the file, but Travis put out a hand to stop her. "Wait a minute. Look at this." He dragged his finger across the touch pad to highlight a paragraph that began at the bottom of the page. "This mentions Fireline Road, see?"

She squinted at the screen. "It says they'll need to extend Fireline Road up over the ridge to provide a second access route to the resort." She looked at Travis. "Does that mean the resort is just over the ridge from the storage facility?"

He nodded. "Which would make it easy for anyone on the ridge to keep an eye on the storage facility, too. Maybe whoever shot Eddie was on Hake's land and saw Eddie from there."

"That still doesn't tell us why they would do something like that."

"No, but I think first thing tomorrow I'll drive to the resort property and see if it looks like anyone has been up there. Henry Hake said the group is restructuring, so I wouldn't think there would be any work going on."

"Don't go by yourself," she said.

"No. I'll take Gage or Dwight with me. And I'll be careful."

She turned back to the computer. "Let's see if there's anything else interesting on here." She scrolled through the list of file names and stopped when she came to a file named jan.

"Jan as in January?" Travis asked.

"Or Jan as in Jan Selkirk?" Lacy opened the file. The first page was a list of dates. 04/06/14, 07/29/14—seventeen different dates altogether.

"Those are all from the months prior to Andy's death," Travis said.

Lacy scrolled to the second page of the file. This one was a photograph. She enlarged the photo on the screen. "That's Jan Selkirk," she said, staring at the wide-mouth brunette who was sitting on the lap of a burly blond man. "She's changed her hair color, but that has to be her. And is that—"

"Henry Hake," Travis said. "Keep scrolling."

The next four pages in the file were more pictures of Jan Selkirk and Henry Hake—the last two of them kissing passionately, his hand up her skirt.

Lacy scrolled until her cursor reached the end of the file. "That's all there is," she said.

"Jan Selkirk is married to Barry Selkirk," Travis said. "She has been for years."

"So Jan and Henry Hake were having an affair?" Lacy stared at the last picture, of the former mayor and the developer locked in a steamy kiss. "This explains why Jan was acting so strangely at Brenda's house this afternoon."

"Strange in what way?"

"She insisted on going into Brenda's basement to retrieve the computer herself, and when I went down to see what was taking her so long, I found her going through a box of things from Andy's office. Then she volunteered to take the computer to the sheriff's office herself. But then you showed up and foiled that plan."

"She must have suspected Andy had something on here that would damage her reputation," Travis said. "Not to mention her marriage."

Lacy looked ill. "Do you think Andy was blackmailing her?" she asked.

"If he was, that might have given her reason to want him dead." Travis tapped the screen. "Notice anything else about these pictures?"

"Her hair—it's dark brown, like mine."

"I don't remember when she changed it, but it may have been about the time Andy died," he said. "We might be able to find pictures in the newspaper archives."

"The woman Wade Tomlinson saw outside Andy's office the day he died—that could have been Jan."

"Maybe so." He tapped the keys to shut down the computer. "I need to take you home," he said. "I have to get this down to the station." He bent down and kissed her cheek. "Sorry we never got around to dinner."

"Oh, I don't know." Her smile sent heat curling through his stomach. "I thought dessert was pretty good."

"Only pretty good?"

"Awfully good." She kissed him on the mouth, then stood. "Let me know what happens with Jan," she said.

"I will. I'd like to put an end to this case as soon as possible."

"Yeah, I hate to think of Jan as a murderer."

"I'm going to make sure of her guilt before I ask the DA to file charges," Travis said. "I want to bring Andy's killer to justice, but I want to be sure we've got the right person this time."

"IF YOU WANT to discuss security for Pioneer Days, I don't see why we couldn't have done so at my office at the museum." Jan Selkirk swept into the Rayford County Sheriff's Department on a wave of expensive perfume, a

ɔright blue Questions? Ask Me! button affixed
ɔ her blouse.

"What's with the button?" Gage asked as he
:scorted her into an interview room.

She glanced down at the four-inch button.
'It's for Pioneer Days. I'm an information
ɪelper. We'll have them stationed through-
ɔut town. Anyone who sees this button knows
hey can approach that person and find out the
:chedule of activities, or where the restrooms
ɪre located or anything else they need to know."

Travis came into the interview room and
:losed the door behind him. Jan's smile faltered.
'Why are we in here?" she asked. "Couldn't we
ʒo in your office?"

"I didn't ask you here to talk about the fes-
.ival," Travis said.

Her color paled beneath her makeup. "What
s going on, Sheriff?" she asked. "I don't have
ime to waste on trivial matters."

"Oh, I don't think this is a trivial matter. Sit
ɪown." He motioned to a seat at the confer-
:nce table, then took the chair across the table
or himself.

Jan hesitated, then sat. She glanced up at
ʒage, who remained standing by the door. "Am
under arrest?" she asked.

"Not at this time. We just want to ask you a
ew questions. You're free to go anytime."

She looked toward the door, as if debating leaving. Travis was gambling that she wouldn't. "I'm going to record the conversation," he said, and switched on the recorder that sat at one end of the table. "That's for your protection, as well as ours."

"You're making me very nervous," she said. "What is this about?"

Travis opened a folder and slid out a stack of photos—three of the pictures taken from Andy Stenson's computer enlarged to eight-by-ten-inch glossies. He arranged the photos in front of Jan. "Recognize these?"

She stared at the pictures, all the color bleached from her face. "Where did you get these?" she whispered.

"They were on Andy Stenson's laptop," Travis said. "You knew they might be there. They're why you tried so hard to get the laptop away from Brenda. I think you planned to destroy the machine, or maybe just erase the files."

"I don't know what you're talking about." But she continued to stare at the photographs, pain reflected in her eyes.

"You were having an affair with Henry Hake," Travis said. "An affair you didn't want your husband and the town council to know about. I looked up some council minutes from that time period and you were one of the strongest supporters for Hake's resort development, urging the council to pass resolutions that would make it easier for him to build his high-altitude luxury homes."

"I supported the development because it was a good idea. Not because I was sleeping with Henry Hake." Her voice was stronger, though the fear hadn't left her eyes.

Travis waited until her eyes met his before he spoke. "Was Andy blackmailing you?" he asked.

"No. Of course not!" She sat back, hands clutching the edge of the table. "You're thinking if he was I would have a good reason to kill him but I didn't kill him, I promise."

"We're going to subpoena your financial records," Travis said. "As well as Andy's bank accounts. They'll show if you were paying him to keep this quiet."

She shifted in her chair, hands clenching and unclenching. "All right—yes. He was blackmailing me. He said he wouldn't tell Barry or anyone else about the affair as long as I paid. He said he needed the money to finish the remodeling on his house. He let Brenda think all the money came from Henry Hake." She laughed, a hysterical sound. "I suppose in a way that was true, since I had to borrow money from Henry to pay Andy. But I didn't kill him. I wouldn't do something like that."

"A slim woman with dark brown hair was seen outside Andy's office about the time he died," Gage said. "We know now that woman wasn't Lacy—was it you?"

"I didn't kill him," she said. "I went there to talk to him—to tell him I couldn't keep paying him. I told him if he didn't stop harassing me I would make Henry Hake cancel his contract with Andy."

"I'm surprised you hadn't thought of that before," Travis said.

She made a face. "Henry didn't really have a say in who represented the development corporation," she said. "He was the public face of the company, but his business partners—the people behind the scenes—made all the decisions. Henry didn't think Andy was experienced enough to represent the group, but his objection was overruled."

"What happened when you went to talk to Andy that day?" Travis asked.

Her mouth tightened. "He laughed at me. He laughed. I didn't say half of what I wanted to say before he started laughing. He said he wasn't about to give up his very lucrative 'side job' and I'd better focus on finding a way to pay. He said Henry wouldn't fire him because he knew things about Henry that his business partners wouldn't want to know."

"What happened then?" Gage leaned over the table toward her. "Did you attack him in a fit of rage? Stab him in the heart with the letter opener he kept on his desk?"

"No! I ran out of there. I left by the back door so no one would see me. I was crying and I didn't want to have to make up some excuse if I ran into anyone."

"So you didn't see anyone when you were leaving?" Travis asked.

"No. The next day I heard Andy had been murdered and I was terrified. You can't imagine my relief when I heard Lacy had been arrested."

Travis tamped down his anger. "You really thought she killed Andy?" he asked.

"I just assumed he had been blackmailing her, too." Jan sniffed. "I wouldn't be surprised if Andy was getting money from other people in town. Everybody thought he was such a nice young man, but he had a sly streak."

"Who else do you think he was blackmailing?" Gage asked. "Besides you and possibly Henry Hake?"

"I don't know." She straightened, some steel back in her spine. "And I've said enough. Too much. I want a lawyer."

Travis slid back his chair and stood. "Call him. You can wait for him in here." He and Gage left the room, locking the door behind them.

Outside, at the end of the hallway, the brothers conferred. "What do you think?" Travis asked.

"She admits she was in Andy's office that day," Gage said. "It had to have been only minutes before he died. She's got a motive, since he was threatening to tell her husband about the affair."

"I don't think it's enough to hold her," Travis said.

"If we don't arrest her, she's liable to leave town and try to disappear," Gage said. "She's got money and I bet she's got a passport."

"I wish we had more evidence against her."

"You're afraid of making the same mistake with her you made with Lacy," Gage said. "That isn't going to happen a second time."

"Let me call the DA, see what he says," Travis said.

The DA agreed with Travis that they probably didn't have enough evidence to arrest Jan at this time, but that she was a strong suspect. By this time both Barry Selkirk and the lawyer Jan had hired to represent her had arrived at the police station.

"My client—"

"My wife—"

Travis waved away the attorney and the husband's protests. "You're free to go, Jan," he said. "But I'll need you to stay close, in case I have more questions."

"I get it. Don't leave town." She stood, gathering her dignity. "Obviously, I've done some things I'm not proud of." She slanted a look at her husband. "But I did not kill Andy Stenson."

They watched her walk out of the door, flanked by her lawyer and her husband. "Do you believe her?" Gage asked.

"Yeah." Travis shoved his hands in his pockets, shoulders hunched. "Right now, anyway, I do."

"So what now?"

"I'm going to talk to Henry Hake and I'm going to check out the site of Eagle Mountain Resort. Why don't you search through Andy's computer and see if you can find anyone else he was blackmailing?"

"We might end up with a whole town full of suspects," Gage said.

"The only one I care about is the person who really killed him," Travis said. "Find him or her and we'll tie up a whole lot of loose ends."

BLACKMAIL! AND JAN SELKIRK? I just can't believe it." Brenda sat between Lacy and Jeanette

Milligan on the Milligans' sofa, a cup of coffee steadied on one knee.

"I was shocked, too," Lacy said. "I never would have believed Andy would do something like that. I knew he was doing better financially, but he told me you had inherited a little money from a favorite aunt, and that was enough for you to finish the remodeling on your house."

"I thought the money came from Henry Hake and the other new clients he had." Brenda sipped her coffee. Her eyes were red and puffy, and Lacy knew she must have been mourning this new revelation about her husband. "I thought I knew him so well," she said. "And to think all this time he was lying." Her voice caught on the last word and she bowed her head.

Jeanette pulled her close and handed her several tissues. "Andy was misguided, but he loved you," she said. "That's what you have to remember."

"Mom is right." Lacy patted Brenda's hand. "Andy did love you. I never knew him to ever look twice at another woman."

Brenda nodded and raised her head. "To think I've worked with Jan all this time and never knew she cheated on her husband. But can't believe she killed Andy over it."

"I'm shocked, too," Lacy said. "Of course, I don't know her well, but the way Andy died—it never struck me as something a woman would do. It was just so…brutal." She glanced at Brenda. "Sorry. I shouldn't have said that."

"No, it's okay," Brenda said. "It *was* brutal. The trial kind of numbed me to the whole thing, but I agree. It never set well with me when the prosecutor said Andy was killed by a woman. For one thing, he was a young, strong guy. You and Jan Selkirk just aren't big, physical women. I think Andy could have fought her off easily."

"I've been trying to think if there was anyone else Andy might have been trying to get money from," Lacy said. "Someone besides Jan who might have had a reason to kill him. There's Henry Hake, of course. He might not have wanted news of the affair getting out, and he certainly had a lot more money than Jan."

"I'm sure Travis has already thought of that," Jeanette said.

"Speaking of Travis." Brenda sat up straighter and dabbed at her eyes. "I don't think I was imagining the sparks flying between the two of you yesterday when he picked you up at my house."

"He canceled dinner with us in favor of a *private* dinner with Lacy," Jeanette said. "Though come to think of it, when she came in several

hours later, she said she was starved becaus
they had never gotten around to eating."

"Hmm. I wonder what two people could d
for several hours that would make them forge
all about food?" Brenda said.

Lacy's cheeks burned and she refused to loo
her mother or Brenda in the eye. "Travis and
have gotten close," she said.

Jeanette covered her ears. "I don't think
want to hear any more." She lowered her hand
and smiled. "But your father and I think he'
a very nice young man. And it's good to se
you so happy."

"If anyone deserves it, you do," Brenda saic

"You deserve to be happy, too," Lacy saic
"I'm so sorry about Andy. It feels as if he die
all over again."

"There's something else about all this that'
bothering me," Brenda said.

"What's that?" Lacy asked.

"Do the police think Jan is the person wh
ran us off the road in that truck, then burne
the truck, and blew up the storage unit whil
you and Travis were inside?" Brenda asked
"And if she was, who shot Eddie Carstairs? Ja
was with me when that happened—and the
the two of us were with you."

Lacy stared at her. "I've been so focused o

an as a suspect in Andy's murder that I didn't think of that," she said.

"If she could kill Andy, she might not hesitate to kill you or anyone else who threatened her," Jeanette said.

"Yes, but with a big truck?" Brenda asked. "Or a bomb? What does Jan know about trucks or bombs? And then she sets the truck on fire and hikes home cross-country?"

"I don't know her as well as you do, but I can't picture her doing any of that," Lacy said. She put a hand over her stomach, which felt as if she had eaten way too much pie. "I hope Travis isn't making another mistake."

"You should call and talk to him," Brenda said. "Not that you should tell him how to do his job, but maybe he'll put your mind at ease. He might have an explanation that we haven't thought of yet."

"Or maybe he thinks Jan had an accomplice or something," Lacy said. She slipped her phone from her pocket and tapped in Travis's cell number. After two rings the call went to voice mail. "Call me when you get a chance," she said, hesitant to say more—especially with Brenda and her mother listening in.

Brenda set aside her half-empty coffee cup and stood. "Thanks for letting me vent," she said. "I have to get to work."

"The museum is open, even with Jan unde suspicion?" Jeanette asked.

"Oh, yes. We're redoing all the displays an adding new ones for Pioneer Days." She picke up her purse and slung the strap over her shou der. "It's coming up quickly, so I'd better g busy."

"I can help." Lacy stood, also. "I don't kno the first thing about history, but I can put thing where you tell me," she said. "Consider me you newest volunteer."

"That's the best offer I've had all day, Brenda said.

Jeanette rose and walked with them to th door. "If Travis stops by, I'll let him kno you're at the museum," she said.

"Mom, you don't have to be my person secretary."

"I know this is a little awkward," Jeanett said. "After all, you're not a teenager anymor But just so we won't worry, if you're going t stay out overnight, text and let us know you'r safe."

"Umm. Okay."

Lacy followed Brenda out to her car. "Di your mom just give you permission to spen the night with Travis?" Brenda asked.

"Yes. Talk about awkward!" Lacy rolled he

eyes. She could joke about it with Brenda, but she added "look for own apartment" to the top of her to-do list.

THE BIG IRON gate across Henry Hake's drive stood wide-open when Travis visited the house later that day. The sheriff parked in the paved circular drive and walked up to the massive oak entry doors. He rang the bell three times, but received no answer. No one answered when he called Henry Hake's private number, either.

Travis walked around the house, peering in windows, his boots crunching on the heavy layer of bark mulch in the immaculately tended landscape. Hake didn't strike Travis as the type to want to get his hands dirty, so he imagined an army of gardeners tending the lilacs and creeping juniper. The garage had no windows, so Travis couldn't tell if a car was parked inside, but the house itself had a deserted look, with no lights showing from within.

He returned to his vehicle and called the office of Hake Development. "This is Rayford County Sheriff Travis Walker," he told the woman who answered. "I'm out at Henry Hake's house and he doesn't appear to be home. It's important that I reach him."

"I'll put you through to Mr. Hake's adminis-

trative assistant," the woman on the other en
of the line said.

Seconds later, the brisk woman Travis ha
spoken with before answered. Travis intro
duced himself once more. "It's very importar
that I speak with Mr. Hake," he said.

"You're from the police, you say?"

"The sheriff's office, in Rayford County
where Mr. Hake lives. I believe we spoke th
other day. I'm at Mr. Hake's house now and h
isn't home."

"Yes, I remember speaking with you. I wa
thinking I should call you later today, if I hadn
heard from Mr. Hake," she said.

"What about?" Travis asked.

"I'm afraid I can't tell you where Mr. Hak
is right now, because I don't know. I haven'
heard from him in a couple of days, and I'r
starting to get worried."

"Does he often disappear without telling yo
where he's going?" Travis asked.

"Oh, no. He always stays in touch. That'
why this is so unusual. And why I was goin
to call you."

"I'm not sure I understand," Travis saic
"Do you think something has happened to M
Hake?"

"I couldn't say. All I know is that Mr. Hak
is missing."

Chapter Fifteen

Volunteering at the history museum was not the most exciting work Lacy had ever done, but she enjoyed spending time with Brenda, and the work gave her something to do. Now that she had adjusted to life at home once more, she was growing restless. She needed a job, but a small town like Eagle Mountain didn't offer many employment opportunities, so for now at least, volunteering seemed the best solution.

The museum occupied the building that had once been Eagle Mountain's hospital, back at the turn of the nineteenth century, when the town had boasted five grocery stores, a dairy, a lumberyard, a train depot and a population five times what it was these days. The various rooms of the hospital housed themed displays, with space in the back for a classroom, archives and a workroom. Everyone from schoolchildren to tourists regularly filed through the building, which had developed a reputation as one of th finest small-town museums in the state.

Lacy finished tacking red, white and blu bunting around the large front windows an turned to find Brenda frowning at a compute screen behind the front desk. "What are yo looking at that put that sour look on your face? she asked.

Brenda turned away from the computer. "/ customer came in yesterday, asking about book we usually keep in stock, but were ou of. I was trying to see if I could find out wher Jan orders our books so I could get this lady copy, but I'm having a hard time figuring ou her system for organizing things."

"What will happen if Jan is arrested?" Lac asked, joining her friend at the museum's fror counter, which served as both check-in des and retail checkout.

"Even if she didn't kill Andy—and I sti can't believe she did—her affair will be a scan dal," Brenda said. "The town owns this mu seum and I doubt if they'll keep her on."

"Will you apply to be the director, then?"

"I'd like to." She studied Lacy's face. "Wha about you? Want to be my assistant?"

"I would love to work for you, but I'm not i love with history the way you are." Lacy picke up an antique paperweight from the counter an

rned it over in her hand. "I think I should use
e money I got from the state to go to school."

"Do you know what kind of career you want
pursue?" Brenda asked.

"I was thinking maybe…education. My mom
a teacher and I like kids." She set the paper-
eight back on the counter. "I think I'd be good
the job."

"We certainly need good teachers. You
ould go for it."

"I already did some research," Lacy said.
I can enroll in the university in Junction and
ommute to classes from here."

"So you'd stay in Eagle Mountain?"

"This is home." Even with everything that
ad happened here—the tragedy of Andy's
eath and those awful months before and dur-
g her trial—Lacy still felt more comfortable
ere than she had anywhere else. "I don't want
leave."

"And a certain handsome sheriff is here…"
renda's eyes sparkled.

Lacy laughed. "There is that. But I think I'd
ke to find my own place to live. My parents
re happy to have me stay with them as long
s I like, but it feels too much like I'm in high
chool, with them watching my every move."

"I know a place you can rent," Brenda said.

That got Lacy's attention. Rentals, like jobs,

were scarce in small towns like Eagle Moun
tain. "Where?"

"Andy and I fixed up an apartment over ou
garage, thinking we would use it when relative
visited. It's been sitting empty all this time, bu
I'd love to rent it to you. You'd have your ow
entrance and could come and go as you please

"That sounds perfect." Lacy leaned over th
counter to hug her friend. "Just tell me when
can move in."

Brenda returned the hug. "You should look a
the place first, make sure it's what you want,
she said.

"Does it have room for a bed and my ow
bathroom?"

"And a tiny kitchen and living room," Brend
said.

"Then I love it already."

The bell on the front door rang, announcin
someone had entered the museum. "I'll tak
care of this," Brenda said. "Would you go int
the workroom and look in the closet and tak
out the box marked Pioneer Days Costumes
We need to go through those before the festi
val."

Lacy found the box in question and looke
around for a pair of scissors to cut the tape. Bu
voices from the front of the museum caugh
her attention and she froze, listening. "I didn

know you were interested in local history, Mr. Barnes," Brenda said.

Lacy tiptoed to the door of the workroom and peered out at the front reception area. Ian Barnes, his black Eagle Mountain Outfitters T-shirt stretched like a second skin over his powerful chest and shoulders, stood across from Brenda at the front counter. "Somebody told me you have a display of old climbing gear and some pictures," he said.

Brenda handed him some change and an admission token. "We do. It's in the Local Sports room—second door on the left." She indicated the hallway to her right.

Ian replaced his wallet in his back pocket. "Hello, Lacy," he said.

Lacy jumped. She hadn't realized she was standing where Ian could see her. Reluctantly, she stepped into the front room. "Hello," she said.

"Do you work here, too?" Ian asked.

"No. I'm, uh, volunteering."

He put his hand lightly at her back—a touch that sent a shiver up her spine. "Why don't you show me where this Local Sports room is?"

"Go ahead and go with him, Lacy," Brenda said.

"It's down this way." Lacy hurried forward, away from his touch, and led him to the room, which, in addition to historic photos of rock climbers and skiers, included a feature on a 1930s boxing champion who had hailed from the area and jerseys from local sports teams.

Ian stepped inside the room and Lacy turned to leave, but he grabbed her by the wrist. "Stay a minute and tell me more about yourself," he said.

She pressed her back against the door frame, tamping down the urge to flee. Why did this man leave her feeling so unsettled? While every other woman in town seemed gone over the fact that he was so good-looking, what she felt in his presence wasn't attraction, but fear. "Why do you want to know about me?" she asked, keeping her voice light and focusing her gaze on the displays in the room.

"Oh, the usual reason." He smiled, and the effect was dazzling.

"What is the usual reason?"

"I'm a single guy, you're a pretty single woman." He leaned toward her, one hand on the doorjamb, over her head. "I'd like to get to know you better."

"I'm involved with someone, Mr. Barnes," she said, wincing inwardly at the primness of her words.

"The county sheriff. I've seen you two together. But you're not engaged or anything, right?"

"No."

He flashed the smile again. "Then you can't blame a guy for trying." To her great relief, he lowered his hand and turned to study the sepia-toned pictures of men in woolen knickers and heavy boots climbing up Dakota Ridge. "Somebody told me you used to work for that lawyer who was killed."

"Yes."

"I guess you knew all about all his clients then."

"Actually, no, I didn't." She edged toward the door. Why was he asking about Andy's clients?

"I think maybe you know more than you're saying," he said. "That's good. It's always good to know when to keep a secret."

The skin along Lacy's arms stood up in gooseflesh. Did Ian Barnes know about the blackmail? Had Andy blackmailed *him*? She backed out of the room. "I don't have anything to say to you or anyone else," she said.

"That's good." He turned and his eyes met hers, and the look in them froze her blood. His earlier flirtatiousness had been replaced by pure menace. "If I were you, I wouldn't tell my boyfriend, the sheriff, about our little conversation," he said. "After all, your parents have suffered enough, haven't they?"

Lacy all but ran back to the front room, past

Brenda and into the workroom. Brenda hurried
after her. "Lacy, what is it?" she asked. "You're
white as a ghost. Did Ian do something to upset
you? Should I call Travis?"

Lacy shook her head. "No. No, I'm fine.
just…" She put a hand to her head. "I just had
a dizzy spell. I didn't eat breakfast this morning." She struggled to pull herself together, not
to let her friend see how terrified she was. She
felt confident enough to stand up to someone
like Ian Barnes on her own. But when he threatened her family, he left her defenseless.

"Have some water." Brenda took a bottle
from a small refrigerator under the counter and
handed it to Lacy. "Are you sure this doesn't
have something to do with Ian?"

Lacy drank some water and began to feel a
little steadier. "He just makes me uncomfortable, that's all," she said.

"Yeah, he may be gorgeous, but have you
noticed he never smiles?"

Lacy shuddered as she remembered the smile
he had fixed on her like a weapon. "I don't like
him," she said, keeping her voice low.

"I'm sorry," Brenda said. "If he comes around
again, I'll offer to give him a tour myself." She
moved back up front and Lacy sagged against
the counter and drank more water. Should she
tell Travis about her encounter with Ian? Maybe

he could find something on Andy's computer that would point to Ian as the victim of blackmail.

But what if word got back to Ian that she had told, and he made good on his threat to hurt her parents? Travis would offer to protect her family, but what if he couldn't?

"That's funny." Brenda came back into the workroom. "Ian left already."

"Did he say anything?" Lacy asked.

"No. When I walked back into the front room just now he was headed out. I called after him, but he must not have heard me. He got in that Jeep of his and drove away." She shrugged. "I guess all he wanted to see was the climbing gear and pictures. Some people are like that—they're only interested in items related to their hobby or history or family or whatever."

"Right." Lacy finished her water and tossed the bottle in the recycling bin. "I guess we'd better get back to work," she said. "What's next on the list?"

"Costumes." Brenda walked to the box Lacy had taken from the closet, opened it and pulled out a blue-and-white striped dress. Or, Lacy thought it was a dress—until she saw the attached bloomers.

"What is that?" she asked.

"It's an 1890s bathing costume." Brenda held

the garment up to her body. "It's wool, and comes complete with a lace-trimmed cap and lace-up slippers. Jan and I wore them last year for Pioneer Days and they were a hit."

"You'll look adorable," Lacy said, trying hard not to laugh at the image she had of Brenda in the old-fashioned garment.

"Oh, I won't be alone." Brenda reached into the box and pulled out a second costume—this one red, with white ruffles at the neck and hem. "You and Jan are about the same size." She tossed the suit to Lacy. "And don't you dare say no. You promised to help, remember?"

"So I did." Lacy held the bathing costume at arm's length and made a face. It reminded her of a flannel nightgown. Not exactly the thing to turn the head of a certain sheriff.

"Please, Lacy," Brenda pleaded. "Don't make me look ridiculous all by myself. And I could really use the help."

"I'll wear it," Lacy said. "After all, you're going to be renting me my sweet new apartment." And at least volunteering at the festival would help take her mind off Ian Barnes. When she had a little more distance from her encounter with him, she would decide what to do.

TRAVIS SUMMONED HIS DEPUTIES, both regular and reserve, to the sheriff's department for a strategy session. "Eddie is out of the hospital but on medical leave," he said to begin the meeting. "Which may be permanent leave, when I've had more time to review his conduct that day. I don't need reserve officers who decide to interfere with investigations—on their days off or any other time." The pointed look he gave the two other reserve officers in attendance was enough to make them squirm.

"On to the next item of business," he continued. "Pioneer Days is this weekend. The sheriff's office has agreed to supply a couple of officers to help with crowd and traffic control, but four of us will be on duty throughout the weekend, and available to head off trouble if we see it developing."

"Check your schedules," Gage said to the reserves. "With Eddie out, I had to juggle things a bit."

"Moving on." Travis consulted his notes. "Henry Hake's administrative assistant, Marsha Caldwell, filed a missing person's report on him this morning. No one has seen or heard from him in the last forty-eight hours. There's no activity on his phone or credit cards, and his car is missing. But there's no sign of a struggle or violence at his home or office, so it's still possible he took a trip somewhere without telling anyone. He wouldn't be the first company executive to decide to take a break and shut off his phone for a long weekend."

"But you don't really think that's what happened," Gage said.

"No. Everything we've been dealing with lately—the reopening of the investigation into Andy Stenson's murder, the attack on Brenda and Lacy, the bombing of the storage unit, even Eddie's shooting—all have connections to Eagle Mountain Resort. We need to keep digging and see how they all link up."

"What's the next step?" Dwight asked.

"I want to check out the site Hake had planned for his resort. And I want you and Gage to go with me."

The meeting ended a few minutes later. The reserve officers left. Adelaide met Travis, Gage and Dwight in the front office. "It's a wonder your ears aren't burning, considering how the revelation that Andy Stenson was blackmailing Jan Selkirk, and Henry Hake's disappearance are all anybody can talk about."

"Anybody else confess to having been blackmailed by Andy Stenson?" Gage asked.

"Nah. Though Josh Lindberg at the hardware store is supposedly taking bets on whether Henry Hake left town because of the scandal with Jan, or whether Barry Selkirk ran him out of the county."

"That doesn't sound like Barry's style to me," Dwight said. "My guess is he'd be more likely to run Jan out of town."

"Word is he's sticking by her," Adelaide said. "Paid for a top lawyer from Denver and everything."

"I hope they work it out," Travis said. "We're headed up to the resort site to check things out. You know how to reach us if anything happens."

"I'd say we've had more than enough happen lately," Adelaide said. "I'm ready for the crime wave to be over. People are going to get the wrong idea about Eagle Mountain if this keeps up."

They set out, Gage and Dwight together in the SUV, Travis leading the way in the Toyota. The town was abuzz with preparations for the festival the following day. Wade Tomlinson and Brock Ryan were setting up a climbing wall for kids in front of Eagle Mountain Outfitters, and the Elks Club members were transforming the park into a mini-carnival, complete with a test-your-strength game, designed to look like a pioneer chopping wood, and a series of water troughs set up so that kids could pan for gold.

Travis had heard that Lacy was helping Brenda at the museum, but he hadn't had a chance to talk to her, what with the craziness

of Jan's confession that she was blackmaile
and Henry Hake's disappearance. But they ha
made a date to meet up the day of the festiv;
to watch the fireworks together. And maybe
he thought, go back to his place afterward an
make a few fireworks of their own.

The proposed site for Eagle Mountain Reso
was eight miles out of the town proper, nea
the top of Dakota Ridge, but Eagle Mountai
had annexed the land three years previousl;
largely at the urging of then-mayor Jan Se
kirk, on the theory that the luxury developmei
would be a tax boon to the community. So fa
that prediction hadn't come true. The sheriff'
department vehicles drove through the twi
stone pillars that marked the entrance to th
resort, into a landscape of crumbling aspha
and abandoned building foundations. Grass an
even small shrubs broke through the neglecte
streets, and the stakes marking lot lines ha
fallen over or were barely visible through th
underbrush that had taken over. Staked tree
and other landscaping that had died from nt
glect dotted the landscape.

They parked in front of a five-foot-by-fou
foot sign that touted the amenities of the resor
with an artist's rendering of the developmen
the homes all soaring redwood beams and glas

walls, luxury four-wheel-drive vehicles parked
n cobblestone drives while elegantly dressed
men and women smiled and laughed.

"Yeah, it sure doesn't look anything like that
now," Gage observed.

"I never could understand how Hake thought
he was going to sell a bunch of people on living way up here," Dwight said. "It's eight miles
down the mountain to town, and in winter you
could end up stuck up here for days. Not to
mention the avalanche potential." He looked
behind them, up the slope of Dakota Ridge.

"These aren't the kinds of homes people live
in full-time," Gage said. He indicated the il-
lustration on the sign. "People who build these
kinds of places spend a few weeks in them at a
time. When the weather gets bad they move to
their villa in Tuscany or something."

"Let's take a look around," Travis said. He
began walking, heading for a trio of curved
metal air vents jutting up from a concrete pad.

"Looks like air vents," Dwight said. "Maybe
venting an old mine, or an underground utility
plant for the development."

"Maybe," Travis agreed. "They don't look
that old, but maybe putting them in was one
of the environmental requirements for build-

ing up here. Some of these old mines contai
trapped gasses they might have had to vent."

"What exactly are we looking for?" Gag
asked.

"Any signs of recent activity," Travis said. "
have a feeling whoever shot Eddie may hav
been coming from here."

"So you're thinking the shooting didn't hav
anything to do with the storage units?" Gag
said.

"There wasn't any reason to shoot a man f
digging through the ashes of a burned-out sto
age room," Travis said. "The fire destroyed e
erything, which even a casual observer coul
see. But if someone was coming over the ridg
from this area—with something they didn
want anyone else to see—then they might b
willing to kill for it."

The two brothers walked together along th
development's main street, while Dwight ex
plored among the foundations of building
"What does Eddie say about the shooter?
Gage asked.

"He doesn't remember anything," Trav
said. "The knock on the head and the resulta
concussion wiped out his short-term memor
He can't help us."

Mixed in among the modern foundations an
survey markers were the signs of older occupa

ion—weathered timbers with square iron nails
nd bent rusted spikes marked the path of tram
ines that had carried raw ore from the mines.
A new iron gate blocked the opening of a mine
dit that had probably been constructed a hun-
red and fifty years before, and a rusting ore
ar positioned alongside the already-crumbling
oncrete foundation hinted at a future purpose
s a flower planter.

"I may have something over here," Dwight
alled, about fifteen minutes into their search.

Gage and Travis joined him at the end of one
f the streets, where the crumbling blacktop
ave way to drying mud. Dwight pointed to a
air of impressions in the ground.

"Boots," Gage observed and squatted down
or a closer look. "Some kind of work boots,
r heavy-duty hiking boots."

"Army boots," Dwight said. "About a size
hirteen from the looks of them. I've got the
tuff in my unit to make casts of them if you
vant."

"Go ahead," Travis said. He walked from
he mud in the direction of the storage units.
ive feet farther on, he found a heel print that
natched the boot print. Ten yards from there,
e stood on a ledge that overlooked the storage
acility and the end of Fireline Road.

"Sometimes you do know what you're doing,"

Gage said. He studied the ground at their feet. "I don't suppose we'd get lucky enough to find some shell casings."

"I think we're dealing with a pro," Travis said. "Someone who doesn't leave clues behind."

"The footprints were a mistake," Gage said.

"A mistake, or he knows they're not going to give us anything useful."

"It wasn't Jan Selkirk," Gage said.

"She was with Brenda when Eddie was shot," Travis said. "I'm not ruling her out for the murder, but not this. This was someone else."

"Come look at this." Dwight called them over.

On the back of a low rock wall that marked the boundary of the proposed resort, he had located tire imprints. "It's a good-sized truck," he said. "Not a tractor-trailer rig, but maybe a box truck. The tread pattern is still really sharp—they haven't had time to erode in the weather."

"So we know someone was up here," Travis said. He scanned the desolate surroundings. No trees grew taller than four feet, and the wind blew constantly. In summer, the sun burned through the thin air, fading paint, weathering wood and carrying an increased risk of skin cancer to anyone who stayed out in it very long. In winter, nighttime temperatures plunged to

irty below zero and snow piled up in drifts
s tall as two-story buildings. Yes, the views
ere breathtaking, the air clear and the night-
me vista of stars unparalleled, but it seemed
 Travis there were some places where it was
etter for people to visit and not try to domi-
ate entirely.

They spent another half hour exploring the
lace, taking pictures and impressions of what
ey found. The few buildings that were intact
ere locked with heavy padlocks. "I'd love to
e what's inside there," Travis said after he
ook the door of a metal building half sunk
 the side of a hill. "But I'd say our chances
f getting a warrant to search this place are
retty much nil."

"Then why are we bothering with the im-
ressions?" Gage asked.

"We had cause to come up here, tracking the
ooter," Travis said. "If those impressions turn
p anything, I'll make my case to a judge. But
m not holding my breath we'll find anything."

They piled into their vehicles and headed
ack toward town. Halfway there, Travis got
 call from Adelaide. "That writer, Alvin Ex-
ter, is here in the office, demanding to speak
ith you," she said.

"Tell Mr. Exeter I have nothing to say to him."

"He says you'll want to talk to him," Ade-

laide said. "He says he has information abou
Eddie's shooting."

"Is he telling the truth, or only bluffing?
Travis asked.

"Well…" Adelaide paused, then said. "I don
know what kind of poker player he is, but I'r
thinking you might want to talk to him."

Chapter Sixteen

Lacy had a restless night, replaying her interaction with Ian Barnes over and over again. By morning, she had decided she would tell Travis about Barnes and trust him to protect her and her family while dealing with Barnes's threats.

But when she came down to breakfast, she froze at the sight of a hunk of rusting metal resting in the middle of the kitchen table. She stared at it, a sinking feeling in her stomach that she had seen this artifact somewhere before—and recently. "What is that?" she asked.

"Your father thinks it's a piton," her mother said. "You know, the anchor things they drive into rock for climbers to attach safety lines to."

"Right." Lacy had a clear vision of a display of similar pitons on the wall in the Local Sports room at the history museum. "Where did you get it?" she asked.

Her father picked it up and turned it over in his hand. "The craziest thing—it was on the front porch this morning, right in front of the door. I can't imagine where it came from."

"Some climber probably dropped it in the street or it bounced out of a truck and the person who found it left it at the closest house," her mother said. "Though it looks old, antique, even."

"I thought if you were going to the museum again today you could take it down there," her father said. "Maybe they can use something like that—I sure can't."

Lacy had little doubt that she would find a missing space in the museum's display where, until yesterday afternoon, this exact piton had sat. Ian Barnes had brought it here and left it as a message to her. *I know where you live and I can practically come into your house without you ever knowing*, he was saying. *I can hurt you and the people you love and nothing you can do will stop me.*

"Lacy? Are you all right?" Jeanette put a hand on her daughter's shoulder. "You've gone all pale."

Lacy swallowed the bile that had risen in her throat. "I'm fine." She dropped into her chair at the table and forced a smile. "Nothing a cup of coffee won't fix."

"I'll wrap this up for you to take to the

museum," her father said. "Tell Brenda hello from me."

Lacy had thought she would tell her parents that she had agreed to rent the apartment over Brenda's garage, but she needed to deal with Ian before she took that step. Living alone didn't seem like a good idea with him threatening her—and she needed to be near her parents to keep an eye on them.

"It's wonderful of you to help Brenda out at the museum." Lacy's mother placed a mug of coffee in front of her, then sat across from her. "That was so awful about Jan Selkirk. I couldn't believe it—her and Henry Hake. And Andy Stenson was blackmailing her?" She shook her head. "I couldn't say anything while Brenda was here yesterday, but it just goes to show you never can tell about people. I mean, I never would have thought Andy was a blackmailer, and I certainly wouldn't have picked Jan for a murderer."

"Mom, we don't know that Jan killed Andy," Lacy said. "We, of all people, should know better than to jump to conclusions about something so serious."

"Of course, dear." Jeanette stirred her coffee. "Still, someone killed Andy. I know it wasn't you, but knowing who really did it would finally put an end to all the speculation, and you wouldn't have any doubt hanging over your head. People think I haven't overheard their whispering. To some people you'll never be innocent until someone else is proven guilty."

"I don't care about those people," Lacy said. The only people she cared about were here in this room. And, well, Travis. She was beginning to care a great deal about him. Her gaze shifted once more to the rusted piton lying in the center of the table. She couldn't risk telling Travis about Ian. Not when there was so much at stake. She would never forgive herself if anything happened to her parents. And what if Ian hurt Travis?

She finished her breakfast, collected the piton her father had wrapped up for her and walked to the museum. She tried to slip through the door quietly, though the bell announced her arrival. The front room was empty, so she took the opportunity to tiptoe back to the Local Sports room and replace the piton in the display. By the time she made it back up front, Brenda had emerged from the workroom.

"I thought I heard you come in," Brenda said. "And just in time, too. The printer just delivered a bunch of brochures we have to fold and box up to hand out tomorrow. I'd forgotten Jan ordered them."

"I can definitely help with that," Lacy said,

feigning cheerfulness. Though Brenda was as perfectly groomed and put together as ever, she had dark half-moons under her eyes, as if she, too, hadn't slept well last night. Between her hurt over the news about Andy and worry about her friend, Jan, she had a lot to deal with right now.

The two of them were well into the brochures when the bell over the door rang and Jan sashayed in. "Don't look so shocked to see me," she said. "There's lots of work to be done before tomorrow and until the town council relieves me of my duties, I'm still director of this museum."

She stashed her purse in the filing cabinet and locked the drawer, then turned to face them. "I'm only going to say this once, so pay attention. Brenda, I did not kill your husband. I was furious with him for extorting money from me and threatening to tell Barry about the affair, but really, I was furious with myself for getting into such a mess in the first place. I argued with Andy, but I never, never would have killed him. When I left his office that afternoon he was very much alive."

Brenda's eyes shone with tears. "I believe you," she said.

Jan turned to Lacy. "One of my biggest regrets is that I didn't speak out at your trial, when Wade Tomlinson told everyone he had seen you outside Andy's office that day. But I was too much of a coward. I told myself it didn't matter but I know I could have made a difference to you and I didn't. I don't blame you if you hate me for that."

Lacy told herself she should be angry with Jan, but the once-proud woman looked so pathetic. She seemed to have aged ten years overnight, her usually perfect manicured nails chipped and bitten, her lipstick crooked, her hair hanging limp. Jan would never be one of her favorite people, but she wasn't going to waste time hating her. "I'm through holding grudges," she said. Travis had taught her that lesson, hadn't he?

"What does Barry say?" Brenda asked.

Jan's expression grew more strained. "He's understandably upset, and he's moved into our guesthouse. But he's agreed we should see a counselor, so I'm hoping we can get past this."

"Did you know Henry Hake is missing?" Lacy asked. "I heard it on the news last night."

"I heard it, too," Jan said. "Travis contacted me to see if I knew anything about it. But I haven't seen the man in over a year, and we broke off our relationship before Andy died. That was one of the things I told Andy that day when I went to plead with him. I told Henry I couldn't take the stress and I wanted to try to make things better with Barry." She dropped into the chair behind the front counter. "Henry took the news much better than I expected. To tell you the truth, I was a little insulted that he took it so well. But I think I knew deep down inside that Henry was never really invested in a serious relationship. He's one of those perpetually distracted people—so many irons in the fire, so many deals and meetings. I was a bit of casual entertainment."

An awkward silence stretched between them, until Jan stood and picked up one of the brochures. "I'm not going to let my personal problems get in the way of making Pioneer Days as fabulous as possible. We have a lot of people counting on us."

"Right." Brenda picked up a stack of brochures. "Let's get to work, ladies."

ALVIN EXETER LOOKED as cocky as ever when Adelaide ushered him into Travis's office Friday afternoon, after Travis finally decided to talk to him. The writer offered a firm handshake, then dropped into the chair across from Travis's desk. "You're going to be glad you talked to me, Sheriff," he said. "All I ask in return is an interview for my book to get your side of the story. This is going to be great for both of us."

"I'm not interested in making any deals," Travis said. "If you know something that pertains to my case, you have an obligation to tell me."

"I don't know about that." Exeter pursed his lips. "After all, maybe I'm only speculating. And even if I did see something that might pertain to an investigation you're conducting, it's not a crime to keep it a secret, is it?"

"Then I have to ask myself—why would you say you know something about a shooting involving one of my officers unless you're an accessory to the crime?"

Exeter's mouth tightened. "There's no need to make threats."

Travis glared at the man. The guy really rubbed him the wrong way. "Either tell me what you know or quit wasting my time," he said.

Exeter sat back and crossed one leg over the other. "You suspect Jan Selkirk had something to do with the murder of Andrew Stenson," he said. "Don't deny it. The news is all over town. Her motive was that Stenson was blackmailing her over her affair with Henry Hake."

It was true what people said, Travis thought. You couldn't keep anything secret in a small town.

"So it stands to reason she's your chief suspect in the attack on Brenda Stenson and Lacy Milligan," Exeter continued. "As well as the explosion at the storage units."

"We haven't found any evidence linking her to those crimes," Travis said.

"But what if I could give you evidence?" Exeter uncrossed his legs and scooted to the edge of his chair. "That would be worth something to you, wouldn't it?"

"Get on with it, Exeter. I'm losing patience."

"What if I told you Jan Selkirk had an accomplice?" Exeter said. "A man who has the skills and the background to make him perfectly capable of running two women off the road or blowing up a building. And one who I don't think would hesitate to shoot a cop."

"Who are you talking about?" Travis asked.

Exeter grinned. "Ian Barnes."

Travis's heart beat a little faster at mention of the name. Barnes's military background certainly made him familiar with firearms, and explosives, too. And he had a certain menace about him. But looking tough didn't mean a man had broken the law. "What makes you think Jan and Barnes are working together?" he asked.

"Because I *saw* them. In the bar of the motel where I'm staying. Jan Selkirk was wearing

sunglasses and a black wig, but I know it wa
her. She and Barnes had their heads togeth
in a back booth, and then she handed over
stack of bills to him. He counted the mone
slipped it into his wallet and told her she didr
have anything to worry about—he'd take ca
of things."

"What things?" Travis asked.

"He didn't elaborate, but I'm thinking
might be running those two women off th
road, blowing up the storage unit—and mayt
even shooting a cop."

Travis didn't know whether to be annoyed
intrigued by these revelations. "So you saw tw
people talking and one of them gave the oth
some money," he said. "That doesn't make e
ther one of them guilty of a crime."

Exeter's expression hardened. "It does whe
one of them is a suspect in a murder case."

"Go back to your motel room and dream u
a few more conspiracies, Exeter. Don't wast
any more of my time."

The writer shoved to his feet. "You're n
going to look into this?"

"I know how to do my job," Travis said. "Yo
can leave now."

Exeter glared at Travis, then stormed out c
the office. Adelaide swept in after him. "H
didn't look too happy," she said.

"What's the local gossip about Ian Barnes?" Travis asked.

"Other than that it should be illegal for a man to look so good?" She grinned. "I heard he has PTSD, and that's what makes him so stand-offish. He spends a lot of time in the mountains, climbing. I guess that's his big thing. He's friends with Wade and Brock, over at Eagle Mountain Outfitters. What else do you want to know?"

"Any links between him and Jan Selkirk?"

Adelaide hooted. "In her dreams. I think Jan's a little long in the tooth for Ian."

"Exeter said he saw them together and they were pretty cozy."

"If that's true, then she's more of a cougar than I ever expected," Adelaide said.

Travis rose and moved past Adelaide. "Where are you off to?" she asked.

"I'm going to have a chat with Mr. Barnes."

DWIGHT WAS ON DUTY, so Travis asked him to ride along to the Bear's Den B and B. Paige was clearly surprised to find two cops at her door. "Is there a problem?" she asked.

"We're looking for Ian Barnes," Travis said. "Is he around?"

"He checked out yesterday," she said.

"He wasn't going to stay around for the fe tival?" Dwight asked.

"He had a reservation through next week Paige said. "But he said something had com up and he needed to leave." She shrugged. ' had a waiting list of people who wanted to sta here during the festival, so the early checko didn't hurt me."

"Did he say why, exactly, he had to leave? Travis asked.

"No, and I didn't ask. I believe in respectin people's privacy."

"So it didn't strike you as suspicious that h would leave so suddenly?" Travis asked.

"Work with the public long enough and notl ing people do will surprise you," Paige said. ' thought maybe the idea of the crowds that ar coming to town for the festival was stressin him out, so he decided to leave."

From the B and B, Travis and Dwight heade to Eagle Mountain Outfitters. Wade was mai ning the register and greeted the officers whe they walked in. "No more sign of that shor lifter," he said.

"We're looking for Ian Barnes," Travis sai

"Haven't seen him for a couple of days, Wade said. "I think he was planning on doin some climbs out in Shakes Canyon. I'd hav liked to go with him, but we've been too busy at the store."

"We were just over at the Bear's Den and Paige says he checked out yesterday afternoon," Travis said.

Wade frowned. "He didn't say anything to us. But then again, Ian's a different kind of guy."

"What do you mean by that?" Dwight asked.

"Oh, you know—standoffish. Not much for social niceties. He was probably just ready to leave and decided to go. It's a bummer, though, because he was supposed to help with the fireworks show tomorrow night."

"Why was Barnes helping with the fireworks?" Travis asked.

"Because he had experience with explosives in the military," Wade said. "We thought he'd be a natural to help set up the big fireworks display above town. The fire department and the Elks Club do most of the work, but they were happy to get an experienced volunteer."

"Where do they set up the display?" Dwight asked.

"Up the hills overlooking town. There's a big flat ledge there looking out over the town, with a backdrop of cliffs. The Elks cleared all the brush from the ledge years ago, so it makes the perfect spot to set up the explosives."

"Did Barnes say where he planned to head from here?" Travis asked.

"Nah. Ian doesn't like it when people ask too many questions. He's the kind of guy you have to accept at face value, on his own terms. He's an amazing climber, though. Being around him always ups my game."

They left the store. Out on the sidewalk, Travis studied the row of storefronts decorated for the festival. Tourists were swelling the population of the town and the festival promised to be bigger and better than ever. Not the time he wanted a possible shooter and arsonist on the loose. "Let's go talk to Jan," he said. "See what she knows."

"Where do we find her?" Dwight asked.

"Good question." Travis had assumed she would be at home, but what if her husband had kicked her out? He called the office. "Adelaide, where is Jan Selkirk staying right now?" he asked.

"She's still in her home. Barry moved into the guesthouse," Adelaide said. "But if you're looking for Jan, check the history museum. Amy Welch said she saw her over there this morning."

"Thanks."

They headed to the museum. Sure enough, Jan was there, along with Brenda and Lacy

"Hi, Travis," Lacy said, offering a wan smile. She was pale, with dark circles under her eyes, though the bruises from the accident had begun to fade. The stress of the whole situation with Ian must be getting to her.

He returned the smile, then turned to Jan. "We need to speak with you for a minute," he said.

He could tell she wanted to argue, but appeared to think better of doing so in front of Brenda and Lacy. "Come back here," she said, motioning them to follow her into a room at the back of the building. She shut the door behind them. "I've answered all the questions I'm going to without my lawyer, Sheriff," she said.

"Just tell me where Ian Barnes is headed," Travis said. "He checked out of the B and B yesterday. I want to know where he went."

"How should I know where's he going?"

"Because the two of you are friends, aren't you?"

She looked away.

"I have a witness who saw you with him," Travis pressed. "You were at a motel bar, and you gave Barnes money."

Her face crumpled and she let out a strangled sob. The sudden breakdown of a woman who had always struck Travis as having ice water in her veins was shocking. "What do you have to tell us, Jan?" he asked.

"It wasn't supposed to turn out that way," she said through her tears. "That wasn't what I wanted at all."

"What wasn't what you wanted?" Travis asked. He led her to a chair and gently urged her down in it, then pulled up another chair opposite her, while Dwight stationed himself by the door. "Tell me about Ian Barnes."

She sniffed, and dabbed at her eyes with the tissue Travis handed her. "He was Henry Hake's bodyguard," she said. "I hadn't seen him for years and I didn't recognize him when he first came to town—when I knew him before, he had longer hair and a moustache. And he didn't call himself Ian Barnes then—he was Jim Badger. But he remembered me. He showed up at here at the museum late one evening, when I was working by myself. He said if I knew what was good for me, I wouldn't tell anyone I had known him before."

"Did he say why he was back in the area?"

She shook her head. "No, and I didn't ask."

"What about the money you gave him?"

"I think I'd better call my lawyer," she said.

"Call him," Travis said. "But I'm warning you now that when I find Barnes, I'm arrest-

ng him. If I find out you gave him money and
e's involved in any of the other crimes I'm
'ying to solve—including the attack on Lacy
nd Brenda and the shooting of my deputy, I'll
harge you as an accessory to attempted mur-
er—and possibly murder." The threat was a
luff. While his suspicions were growing that
'arnes was involved in the recent spate of local
rimes—and maybe even Andy Stenson's mur-
er—Travis didn't yet have enough proof to ac-
ually arrest him.

"I didn't have anything to do with any of
hose things," Jan said. She bit her lower lip so
ard it bled.

Travis softened his voice. "If you need to tell
ne something, you should do it now," he said.

She glanced toward Dwight, then shifted her
aze back to Travis. "All right, I did give him
noney. I paid him to burn down the storage
nit. I wanted to be sure Andy's files were de-
troyed, so that you wouldn't find out about
ny affair with Henry. He said he could set a
re and no one would ever figure out who did
. I didn't know he was going to put a bomb
ut there—or that you and Lacy would end
p hurt." She grew more agitated. "I swear I
idn't know."

Travis stood. "Call your lawyer," he said.

"Then I want you both to report to the sheriff's department. Turn yourself in and we'll talk to the DA about the charges."

He left her sobbing, with Dwight standing guard. Lacy met him outside the door. "What is going on?" she asked. "Is that Jan crying in there?"

"She's going to be all right," Travis said. "Are you okay?"

"A little stressed," she said, still watching the door to the workroom.

"It will all be over soon," Travis said. He touched her arm. "I can't say more, but trust me."

Her gaze met his and she nodded. More than anything just then, he wanted to kiss her, but the timing felt off. "I do trust you," she said.

"We're still on for the fireworks tomorrow night, right?" he said.

"Yes. I'm looking forward to it." Then she stood on tiptoe and gave him a quick kiss on the lips—a firm, warm pressure that sent a jolt of electricity through him. But before he could reach out and pull her closer, she had moved away. "I'd better let you get back to work," she said, and left the room.

But she had given him a good reminder of how much she was coming to mean to him

nd of how much he wanted to clear this case,
o that there would be nothing holding them
ack in the future.

Chapter Seventeen

Pioneer Days Festival in Eagle Mountain fea-
tured the kind of weather Coloradans love t
brag about—balmy air, gentle breezes and
sky the color of blue china glaze, a few cot-
tony clouds hanging around as if for the sol-
purpose of adding interest to photographs o
the scenery. As it was, Lacy found herself pa
of that scenery. In her 1890s bathing costume
she handed out sugar cookies and lemonad-
and posed for photographs with families, chi
dren and a few grinning young men who flirte
shamelessly but were otherwise harmless.

Crowds of people showed up to tour the museum, keeping Brenda and Lacy busy. Neithe
of them had seen or heard anything from Ja
who had left the museum the day before with
out saying a word. For once the town rumc
mill wasn't churning with any informatio
about the former mayor. Nobody had hear
anything about her.

Mayor Larry Rowe made an appearance at the museum midafternoon to shake hands and congratulate everyone on helping to put together such a great festival. "Lacy, you're looking wonderful," he said, accepting a cup of lemonade. "I'm glad to see you're doing so well, making a fresh start."

What else was she supposed to do? she wondered, but she didn't voice the question out loud. She merely smiled and moved on to ladling more lemonade into cups.

Travis stopped by for a few minutes after the mayor left, but Lacy only managed to smile at him from behind the counter where she was pouring lemonade. He waved and moved on, but Lacy felt giddy from the brief encounter.

"You certainly look happy about something." Tammy, the reporter from the *Eagle Mountain Examiner*, focused her camera on Lacy. "Keep smiling like that." She clicked off half a dozen pictures, then studied the preview window of her camera. "Oh, those came out nice," she said. "You look great, and the museum and the crowds in the background might as well be an advertisement for Pioneer Days."

"I had no idea so many people would come to town for this," Lacy said.

"It's a draw," Tammy said. "Though we can thank the weather for the bigger-than-ever turn-

out, I think. And it's supposed to be perfect fo
the fireworks show tonight and, of course, th
dance afterward." She snagged a sugar cooki
from the tray to Lacy's left. "Only bad thin
is that handsome Ian Barnes left town. I wa
hoping to wrangle at least one dance with tha
hunk. I probably wouldn't have worked up th
nerve to ask him, but a girl can dream, right?
She took a bite of cookie.

"Ian left town?" Relief surged through Lacy

"Yeah. Paige said he had reservation
through the end of next week, but he came t
her and said something had come up and he ha
to leave." She brushed cookie crumbs from th
front of her shirt. "I'm thinking somebody tol
him about the crowds this festival attracts an
he figured he didn't want to deal, you know?

Lacy nodded absently. She leaned towar
Tammy, her voice lowered. "Do you know
what's up with Jan Selkirk?" she asked. "W
haven't heard a word from her all day. It's lik
she's disappeared."

"Maybe she and her husband went away fo
a few days," Tammy said. "I heard they wer
trying to patch things up."

"Could she do that?" Lacy asked. "Woul
the sheriff let her leave town while the inves
tigation is still ongoing?"

"I have no idea," Tammy said. "But I'll asl

around. If I hear anything, I'll try to swing back by here and let you know."

"Thanks."

By six o'clock, when the museum closed, Lacy's feet ached and her head throbbed. But Travis had agreed to meet her at seven thirty. They planned to walk to the park and stake out a good spot from which to view the fireworks. They could do a little catching up while they waited for the show to begin, and maybe enjoy a glass of wine and a slice of pizza from one of the vendors in the park.

She walked back to the house without having to stop even once. The crowds had thinned and she guessed most of the tourists were eating supper or had headed to their hotels to change or put their feet up before the fireworks show and dance tonight. She let herself into the house and found a note on the hall table from her mom. "Having dinner with Dick and Patsy Shaw. Will probably get home after you leave. Love, Mom."

Lacy smiled. It was a rare occasion when she had the house to herself. Too bad she didn't have time to enjoy it. She went upstairs and changed into capris and a knit tank with a matching cardigan for after dark, when the air would cool and she'd welcome another layer.

She still had half an hour before Travis would

be here, so she poured a glass of iced tea and
went out into the backyard. Here, where a
wooden fence protected the space from hun-
gry deer, her mother had created a sanctuary
of flowers and fruit. Apple trees full of green
apples gave way to paths lined with colorful
hollyhocks. A copper birdbath and feeders attracted juncos, goldfinches, orioles and other
birds, and wind chimes in the trees added their
melody to the scene.

Lacy decided to pick a hollyhock for her hair
and headed toward a stand of dark pink blos-
soms near the back fence. As she leaned over
to pluck the flower, something rustled in the
bushes. Out of the corner of her eyes, she saw
a flash of movement, then someone grabbed
her from behind. She struggled as something
was pulled over her head, blinding her, and she
was thrown to the ground. "Make a sound and
I swear I'll kill you now." The man's voice was
low, his breath hot against her cheek. Something sharp pricked at the side of her breast and
she sucked in a breath.

"That's right," the voice said. "Keep quiet or
Mommy and Daddy will come home to find
you butchered in their backyard."

AT SHORTLY AFTER SEVEN, Travis met Lacy's parents as they came up the walkway toward their

house. "Are you coming to get Lacy?" Jeanette asked as George unlocked the front door.

"I stopped by the museum on my way over and Brenda said she left about an hour ago to come home and change," he said, following them into the house.

"That old-fashioned swimsuit was so cute on her," Jeanette said. "Though she said the wool was a little itchy. Can you imagine wool for a swimsuit?" She stopped at the bottom of the stairs and called up. "Lacy! Travis is here!"

He waited, but heard no response. "Go on up," George said. "She's probably drying her hair or something and didn't hear you."

Travis climbed the stairs, though he heard no hair dryer or other noise as he neared the door to Lacy's room, which stood open. He paused in the doorway and knocked. "Lacy? Are you in here?" The antique swimsuit lay across the end of the neatly made bed. A laptop sat on her desk near the window, the top open but the machine shut off. Lacy's purse lay next to it, her phone tucked in a side pocket.

He checked the upstairs bathroom, and even peeked into a second bedroom he assumed belonged to her parents, but found no sign of Lacy.

"Did you find her?" Jeanette asked when he joined her and George in the kitchen.

"No. Her purse is on her desk in her room but she's not upstairs."

George frowned. "That's odd. She's no down here." He looked at his wife.

"Maybe she decided to walk over to the park and meet you," Jeanette said.

"She would have taken her purse. Or a least her phone. It's upstairs in her purse." The bad feeling that had started when he had seer Lacy's empty bedroom was growing.

"Oh, this is just silly." Jeanette moved to the back door. "She's probably sitting out here ir the backyard and we're in here worrying."

But the Milligans' backyard was empty and silent, save for the faint sounds of celebration that drifted from the center of town and the gurgle of the creek just past their fence line "Lacy!" Travis shouted.

But no answer came.

"What could have happened to her?" Jeanette clutched her husband's arm.

"She probably did walk downtown to mee me," Travis said, keeping his voice steady and his expression calm. "She's probably still no used to carrying a phone around with her and she forgot it. I'll go look for her."

"Let us know when you find her," George said.

"Of course."

He forced himself not to hurry out of the house, to assume the calm, easygoing saunter of a man who wasn't worried. But as soon as he was out of sight of the Milligans' home, he pulled out his phone and called Gage. "Lacy is missing," he said. "Spread the word to the others to keep an eye out for her."

"What do you mean, 'missing'?" Gage asked.

"She left the museum an hour ago and came home to change," Travis said. "Looks like she did that, but her purse and phone and keys are still here at her parents' house, only she's not."

"She probably just went downtown and forgot her phone," Gage said.

"I hope that's what happened," Travis said. "But I can't shake the feeling she's in trouble."

Ian Barnes had bundled Lacy into his Jeep and driven out of town, away from the crowds of people who might see her with him and act to help her. Once they had reached the vehicle, he had exchanged the knife for a gun and kept it pointed at her while he drove, one-handed, up a dirt road that led up Dakota Ridge.

"Where are you taking me?" she asked, hating the way her voice shook.

"I've been helping the Elks Club set up for the big fireworks show tonight," he said. "They were thrilled to get a guy with my experience with explosives to volunteer. They've cleared off a big ledge for the staging area for the show but there's another ledge above that. Great view of the town, and when all the fireworks start going on, no one will be able to hear you when I kill you."

"Why are you going to kill me?" she asked, struggling to keep the tremor from her voice.

"Because you know too much."

"I don't know anything," she said. "Not anything to do with you."

"Some things you don't realize the significance of, but we can't risk you figuring them out later."

"Who is we?"

He gunned the Jeep up a steep slope, gravel pinging against the undercarriage, tires spinning until he gained traction. "That doesn't matter."

She stared at him, a cold, sick feeling washing over her. "You killed Andy, didn't you?" she asked.

Ian grinned. "I broke into the office while he was at lunch. I knew it was your day off and that he'd be alone. I hadn't counted on Jan coming by to see him, but it was easy enough to hide in the bathroom while she pleaded with him. She left out the back door and before he had time to even move, I stabbed him. He

lidn't suffer. I left by the back door and drove
out of town."

"But why kill him?" she asked. "What did
Andy ever do to you?"

"It was a job." He voice was matter-of-fact,
as if he was talking about moving furniture
or clearing brush. "He was poking his nose
where it didn't belong. The people who hired
me wanted him shut up."

"What was he poking his nose in?" She
couldn't recall anything he had talked about,
but that had been so long ago.

"I don't know and I don't care," Ian said.

"Did Henry Hake hire you?"

He laughed. "That loser? No. Hake had people above him who ran the show. They hired
me."

"Why did you bother coming back to town?
Why now?"

"I had a job to do."

"For the same people who hired you to kill
Andy?"

"Maybe."

"Who are they?"

He glanced at her, his expression cold. "I
don't see that that has anything to do with you."

"Were you the one who tried to run Brenda
and me off the road that day?"

"Yes. I sacrificed a new truck to that one. It

was hard, watching it go up in flames. But I had the old Jeep as backup."

"And the explosion?"

"Yeah, that was me. I miscalculated the delay on the timer, though. I should have set it for just a little longer."

"Did you shoot Travis's officer?"

"I can't tell you all my secrets, can I?" He parked the Jeep against a sheer rock face, shut off the engine, then leaned over and grabbed her by the arm. "Come on. The show starts in less than an hour. I want to be in place before everyone gets here."

TRAVIS PUSHED THROUGH the crowds of tourists and locals in the park, searching for Lacy. Once he thought he caught a glimpse of her dark hair in a group of women, but it turned out to be someone he had never seen before. As he circled the edge of the park, he came upon a group of firemen, climbing into the chief's truck. "Want to come help with the fireworks, Sheriff?" Assistant Fire Chief Tom Reynolds called.

"You don't need me in your way," Travis said.

"Come on," Tom urged. "We're a man short since Ian Barnes left town early."

"He left town?" a short, balding man next to

Tom said. "That's funny, I could have sworn I saw his Jeep go by just a little while ago. I waved, but I guess he didn't see me."

"You saw Ian Barnes?" Travis asked.

"Yeah. I'm sure it was him. He had a woman with him."

Travis's heart pounded. "What did she look like?"

"I didn't see her face, but she had dark brown hair." He grinned. "Odds are, though, that she's a looker. A guy like that can have any woman he wants. My wife got this dazed look on her face every time she saw him."

"Which way was he headed?" Travis asked.

"The way we're going," the man said. "Hey, maybe he decided to stick around and help us and he went on ahead."

"Hey, Travis, where are you going?" Tom called as Travis took off across the park at a run.

Travis already had his phone out, calling Gage. "I think Ian Barnes has Lacy," he said. "They're headed to that hill above town, where the Elks are getting ready to shoot off fireworks. Get Dwight and meet me up there. And alert Highway Patrol in case we need backup." He hung up as soon as his brother acknowledged the information. He had to get to Lacy. He only hoped he wasn't too late.

A LACEWORK PATTERN of glittering lights marked the town of Eagle Mountain, nestled in the valley below an uplift of mountains and cliffs. Lacy looked down at the town from the narrow ledge Ian had brought her to. Travis was down there somewhere, and her parents. They were probably wondering where she was, but she had no way of signaling to them, no way of letting them know what had happened to her.

Closer even than town, fifty feet below on a much larger ledge, a dozen men swarmed around the metal stands and boxes that contained the explosives set up for the fireworks display. If Lacy yelled, would they look up and see her here? Maybe—but if they did look up in response to her shout, likely all they would see was her death as Ian shot her. And then he would escape, driving away in his Jeep before anyone below had time to react.

"Come away from the edge," Ian said, and pulled her back against the cliff face. The gun dug hard into her side. "You don't want to fall, do you? A drop like that could kill you." He chuckled at his own joke, sending an icy tremor through her.

"Why are you doing this?" she asked again. "I haven't done anything to hurt you."

"It's nothing personal," he said. "It's a job. It pays well and it makes use of my talents."

He leaned back against the cliff, his gaze still steady on her. "It's kind of a shame, though. I mean, you just got out of prison and you don't even get to enjoy a month of freedom before it's over. I'm sorry about that."

She looked away. How could she even comment on such an absurd statement?

"I was inside once," he said. "You did three years, right?"

"Yes."

"That's what I did, too. Course, I hear the women's prisons have it better than the men. But it wasn't too bad for me. I had friends inside and I knew how to work the system. You get respect, even inside, being a military veteran, and I never had to worry about anyone messing with me."

"I wouldn't know about that," she said.

"I remember you from before, you know," he said.

"From before what?"

"Before you went inside. When you worked for that lawyer."

"I don't remember you," she said. Surely she would remember if she had met him before.

"You never saw me. That's part of my job, too, not being seen. They won't see me when I kill you, and they won't see me when I leave."

She closed her eyes, not wanting him to read the fear there. Would those be the last words she ever heard?

THE BACK WHEELS of Travis's SUV skidded around a sharp curve as he trailed the fire department truck up the dirt road to the fireworks launch site. A number of men and vehicles were already at the site, their vehicles parked well away from the explosives, behind a protective wall of boulders. Travis drove right into the midst of the men working. "Something wrong, Sheriff?" one man asked, as Travis lowered his SUV's window.

"I'm looking for Ian Barnes," Travis said. "Have you seen him?"

"I haven't." The man looked around. "Anybody seen Ian Barnes?" he called.

"I thought he left town," someone said.

Tom walked up to Travis. "I don't see him or his Jeep," he said. "Maybe Walt was wrong about seeing him."

"I saw him." Walt walked up behind Tom. "But you're right that he's not here."

"Where else could he have gone?" Travis asked.

Both Tom and Walt registered confusion. "I don't know," Tom said. "There's nothing else up here."

Travis scanned the area. The road he had driven up continued past this ledge. "Where does that road go?" he asked.

"It just climbs up a little ways then peters out," Tom said. "There's an old mine site. I've been up there looking for artifacts, but it's pretty picked over. There's an adit, but the tunnel's full of water and the timbers are falling down, so it's not safe to go inside. There are warning signs posted, but no gate."

A flooded mine shaft. The perfect place to dispose of a body. Travis shut off the SUV and got out. "What are you doing?" Tom asked. "You can't just leave your vehicle here—not with the fireworks so close."

"Then you move it." Travis tossed him the keys. "I'm going up there to look around. When Gage and Dwight get here, tell them where I'm at."

"Okay, Sheriff," Tom said.

The noise and activity of the preparations for the fireworks show faded as Travis climbed. He kept to the shadows at the side of the road, moving stealthily, ears tuned to any sounds from above. The trail was steeper up here, and narrower, and Travis breathed hard on the climb. He doubted many people had the nerve to take a vehicle up something this steep, but Barnes apparently hadn't hesitated.

He crested the last rise and spotted Ian's Jeep first, the battered vehicle tucked in next to a cliff face. Freezing, he waited, listening. After a few seconds he heard the low murmur of voices—a man's, and then a woman's. A band tightened around his chest as he recognized Lacy's voice. He couldn't make out her words, but he felt the fear in her tone as a tightness in his own chest.

Travis drew his gun and began moving toward the voices, stealthily, placing one careful step at a time. By the time he reached the front bumper of the Jeep, he could make out the two shadowed figures against the cliff face and stopped.

He apparently hadn't been stealthy enough. "Step out where I can see you and toss your gun on the ground." Ian's voice was calm, the words chilling. "One wrong move and I'll blast her away right now."

Travis tossed the gun to the ground and raised his hands over his head. *Come on, Gage,* he thought. *Bring in the cavalry anytime now.*

"Come over here and stand next to your ladylove," Ian said. "When the fireworks start I can shoot you both. And hurry up. They're almost ready."

At that moment, the first explosions from below shook the air. Lacy gave a cry of alarm and Ian turned to watch the first rockets soar overhead. "Now," he shouted, but before he could turn back to them and fire, Travis rushed him.

"Lacy, run!" Travis shouted.

LACY RAN, BUT not far. She made it only a few feet before she tripped and went sprawling. Gravel dug into her palms and her knees. Shaking with fear, she crawled to the cliff face and sat with her back against the rock wall, watching as Travis and Ian struggled on the ground. The two men rolled, grappling for the gun, while deafening explosions sounded overhead. Flashes of red and blue and gold illuminated the struggle, and bits of paper and ash rained down. Smoke and the smell of gunpowder stung her nose and eyes, but she blinked furiously and tried to keep track of what was happening.

Travis's discarded gun lay a few feet away. She crawled toward it and had almost reached it when a man stepped out of the shadows and scooped it up. "No offense, Lacy, but I'm probably a better shot with this than you are," Gage Walker said, joining her in the shadows.

"Are you alone?" she asked, looking over his shoulder.

"No. I've got Dwight and a couple of Highway Patrol deputies surrounding this place," he

said. "But I'm not sure there's anything any o
us can do right now but wait and hope one o
us can get off a good shot."

Explosions continued to echo off the rocks
Lacy covered her ringing ears, but kept he
eyes fixed on Travis and Ian, who continue
to wrestle, gouging and kicking. In the flashe
of light she thought Travis might be bleedin
from a cut on his cheek, and Ian's shirt wa
torn. They rolled to the edge of the ledge, unti
Travis's feet hung over the edge. Lacy moane
How could he win? He was in good shape, bu
Ian was phenomenal. She remembered Travi
saying he wouldn't want to meet Ian in a darl
alley. What about a dark mountain ledge?

The two men rolled away from the ledge, an
Lacy let out her breath in a rush. Beside her
Gage did the same. She glanced over and sav
that he was kneeling, steadying his gun witl
both hands, keeping it fixed on the two men a
they moved. "All I need is one clear shot," h
said in a lull between explosions.

The next round of volleys began, and the
Travis was on top of Ian. He slammed the othe
man's head into the rocky ground, then lunge
to his feet and staggered back.

"Freeze!" Gage yelled. "One move and I'l
shoot."

"All right." Ian sat up, his hands over his head. "I give up." He struggled to his feet.

"I said freeze!" Gage shouted again, but already Ian had made his move, lunging toward Travis with a roar.

Gage fired, the explosion deafening, and Travis dodged to the side. With a scream that rose above the sound of fireworks and gunfire, Ian dove over the edge, the echo of his cry hanging in the air as he vanished.

Epilogue

"Goodbye, Jan. And good luck." Lacy faced the older woman, who had aged even more in the past few weeks. She had accepted a plea bargain in the charges against her involving her hiring of Ian Barnes to blow up the storage unit, and would serve a minimum of eighteen months in the Denver Women's Correctional Facility.

"It will be tough at first, but obey the rules and you'll get along fine," Lacy said. "Focus on doing your time and coming home."

"It helps a little, knowing you came out all right," Jan said. "I'm sorry again for all the trouble I caused you."

"I'm not worrying about the past anymore," Lacy said. "I'm focusing on the future, and so should you."

"You've got a lot to look forward to." Jan's gaze shifted to the man who stood behind Lacy.

Travis put a hand on Lacy's shoulder and

nodded to Jan. "Good luck," he said. "I'll see
you when you come home."

Jan turned away, and climbed into the sheriff's department van that would transport her to
Denver. Lacy and Travis watched the van drive
away. "I probably shouldn't, but I feel sorry for
her," Lacy said.

"She brought it all on herself," Travis said.
"And she got off lightly, considering."

She turned to face him and he pulled her
close. She sighed—a sound of relief and con-
tentment. "I'm just glad it's all over and you're
all right."

"I'm all right. As for it being over—Henry
Hake is still missing, you know."

In the whirl of activity in the days following
the death of Ian Barnes, Lacy had forgotten all
about the real estate developer. "No one has
heard anything from him?" she asked.

"Not a word. According to the latest from
Adelaide, public opinion is divided on whether
he skipped town to avoid paying debts Eagle
Mountain Resort had run up, or whether something has happened to him."

"Ian said people who were over Hake hired
him to kill Andy," Lacy said. "Who was he
talking about? I thought Henry Hake owned
his own company."

"That's one thing I'm trying to find out,"

Travis said. "Ian may have been talking abou
investors—or maybe Hake had silent partner:
And I'd like to know what Andy was lookin
into that got him killed. Knowing that migh
help me figure out who hired Barnes. Now
that Exeter knows Barnes killed Andy, he ha
turned his focus to Barnes and Hake, as well.

"So there's still a lot of unanswered ques
tions," Lacy said.

"I'm going to find the answers," Travis saic
"It may take time, but I have plenty of that."

"Lacy! Travis!" Lacy looked up to se
Brenda hurrying toward them. "Was that Ja
leaving just now?" Brenda asked, a little out c
breath as she joined them on the sidewalk i
front of the sheriff's department.

"Yes," Travis said. "You just missed her."

"We said our goodbyes yesterday," Brend
said. "Though I meant to be here this mornin
I got delayed at the museum." Brenda was th
new director of the Eagle Mountain Historica
Museum, a job that came with more responsi
bilities, but also a raise. Already, Lacy coul
see her friend blossoming in her new role.

"Have you seen Lacy's new apartment?
Brenda asked Travis. "She's fixed it up so cute.

"I have an invitation to dinner there tonight,
Travis said.

Lacy hoped the blush that warmed he

cheeks wasn't too evident. Now that she was settled into the apartment over Brenda's garage, she had invited Travis over for a little celebration, which she figured—hoped—would lead to him staying the night.

"I'd better get back to work," Travis said. "It was good seeing you, Brenda." He leaned over and kissed Lacy's cheek. "And I'll see you tonight."

"How are your parents taking the move?" Brenda asked, when Travis had disappeared inside the station.

"My mom cried, but then she cries at any change," Lacy said. "Truly, I think they're both happy for me." She and Brenda began walking back toward the museum.

"You may not need the apartment for long, if our county sheriff has a say in the matter," Brenda said.

"We've agreed to take it slowly," Lacy said. "I have a lot of adjustments to make. I start classes in just a few weeks. I'm pretty nervous about that."

"You'll do great." Brenda took her hand and squeezed it. "It's good to see you so happy. You deserve it."

"I'm happier than I ever thought I could be," Lacy said. "While I was in prison, I told myself the key to surviving was to never give up.

Now I know it can be just as important to have someone on the outside who will never give up on you."

"Travis was your someone," Brenda said.

"Yes." Travis Walker was her someone—her only one. The man who had saved her, and the one who had brought her back to herself. A man she thought she could love for a long time—for a lifetime.

* * * * *

Look for the next book in Cindi Myers's
EAGLE MOUNTAIN MURDER MYSTERY
miniseries, AVALANCHE OF TROUBLE,
available next month.

And don't miss the titles in Cindi Myers's
previous miniseries,
THE RANGER BRIGADE:
FAMILY SECRETS:

MURDER IN BLACK CANYON
UNDERCOVER HUSBAND
MANHUNT ON MYSTIC MESA
SOLDIER'S PROMISE
MISSING IN BLUE MESA
STRANDED WITH THE SUSPECT

Available now from Harlequin Intrigue!

Get 4 FREE REWARDS!

We'll send you 2 FREE Books plus 2 FREE Mystery Gifts.

Harlequin Presents® books feature a sensational and sophisticated world of international romance where sinfully tempting heroes ignite passion.

FREE
Value Over
$20

YES! Please send me 2 FREE Harlequin Presents® novels and my 2 FREE gifts (gifts are worth about $10 retail). After receiving them, if I don't wish to receive any more books, I can return the shipping statement marked "cancel." If I don't cancel, I will receive 6 brand-new novels every month and be billed just $4.55 each for the regular-print edition or $5.55 each for the larger-print edition in the U.S., or $5.49 each for the regular-print edition or $5.99 each for the larger-print edition in Canada. That's a savings of at least 11% off the cover price! It's quite a bargain! Shipping and handling is just 50¢ per book in the U.S. and 75¢ per book in Canada*. I understand that accepting the 2 free books and gifts places me under no obligation to buy anything. I can always return a shipment and cancel at any time. The free books and gifts are mine to keep no matter what I decide.

Choose one: ☐ **Harlequin Presents®**
Regular-Print
(106/306 HDN GMYX)

☐ **Harlequin Presents®**
Larger-Print
(176/376 HDN GMYX)

Name (please print)

Address   Apt. #

City   State/Province   Zip/Postal Code

Mail to the **Reader Service:**
IN U.S.A.: P.O. Box 1341, Buffalo, NY 14240-8531
IN CANADA: P.O. Box 603, Fort Erie, Ontario L2A 5X3

Want to try two free books from another series? Call 1-800-873-8635 or visit www.ReaderService.com

3 1333 04717 5771

---

*Terms and prices subject to change without notice. Prices do not include applicable taxes. Sales tax applicable in N.Y. residents will be charged applicable taxes. Offer not valid in Quebec. This offer is limited to one order per household. Not valid for current subscribers to Harlequin Presents books. All orders subject to approval. Credit or debit balances in a customer's account(s) may be offset by any other outstanding balance owed by or to the customer. Please allow 4 to 6 weeks for delivery. Offer available while quantities last.

Your Privacy—The Reader Service is committed to protecting your privacy. Our Privacy Policy is available online at www.ReaderService.com or upon request from the Reader Service. We make a portion of our mailing list available to reputable third parties that offer products we believe may interest you. If you prefer that we not exchange your name with third parties, or if you wish to clarify or modify your communication preferences, please visit us at www.ReaderService.com/consumerschoice or write to us at Reader Service Preference Service, P.O. Box 9062, Buffalo, NY 14240-9062. Include your complete name and address.